THE MATILDA MAN

Phillip Player

ISBN: 978-1-922784-64-3
First published in Australia July 2023
Layout and design by Clark & Mackay.

Printed by Clark and Mackay, Brisbane, Australia

Dedication

To my late mother, the theatrical actress and the Rage of Sydney in 1939, Cynthia Ross.

The Matilda Man was initiated by her as a film screenplay but never completed, so I have attempted to bring her characters to life in this novel.

Acknowledgements

The Matilda Man was originally a concept written in part by my mother, the theatrical actress Cynthia Ross, as a screenplay but sadly passed away before she could complete this project.

I thank my sister, Laura Player, who kept our mother's writings safe throughout the years and consented for me to complete the task of finishing *The Matilda Man* as a novel.

I thank my dear friend of many years, the renowned journalist and crime writer Janet Fife-Yeomans, for her help in making sure I did not bastardise the Queen's English too much.

To my dear friends Barrister Daniel Brezniak, who pushed me along the way to complete the book; the Publican's publican Ron Moss, who took a 'bloody beaut pitcha' of Dobson on the grog; and Rod Ovens, who I drove crazy fixing my computer skills, or rather my lack of them!

Chapter 1

His name was Dobson. He was a "swagman." And as men of his ilk do, he owned little.

Dobson's worldly possessions were a couple of dirty dishwater shirts and a pair of frayed trousers, eating utensils (bent forks and a bone handled knife for eating), a blackened "billy" for boiling water, a set of Boer war medals (not that Dobson ever went to war) and a battered felt hat that he wore to cover what was left of his wispy grey hair. All this he carried in his swag – a long strip of calico wrapped up like a Christmas plum pudding that dangled at the end of a broken gum tree branch.

Although Dobson was an excellent bushman, it was easier for him to survive by cadging food, baccy and grog from hotels and cooks from the outlying cattle stations. What he could not cadge, he stole, which more often than not had him running foul with the law, just as he was doing now.

Having been nicked for palming bar change in the Nullagine Pub, Dobson was making good his escape by heading to the mining town of Marble Bar. The Bar, as it was affectionally known, was a three-day walk, but he need not walk that far, not when twenty miles north was the railway line. And today, the weekly train was coming through and he intended to be on it.

Gerard Ward, a journalist from the *Fremantle Gazette*, a Perth-based newspaper, was a passenger on that train and had been sent by his newspaper to open an office in Marble Bar, a town renowned as being the roughest and hottest hellhole in Australia. He had secured a first-class ticket, only to find the compartment he was travelling in was cramped and stuffy. His side window refused to close, and he was continually buffeted with hot air mixed with the train smoke that blew in. Sitting across from him was obviously a well-seasoned traveller around these parts.

The Very Reverend George Stoner was dressed more appropriately, though not perhaps for his calling in life. Decked out in loose-fitting cotton trousers and an open-necked shirt, he showed little effect from the heat. Except for a few beads of sweat occasionally dripping from his brow, he looked remarkable fresh, making Gerard look rather foolish sweltering in his woollen suit.

Since boarding the train in Port Hedland, the Reverend had zealously chewed off Gerard's ear about all the good works he had performed in the name of Our Lord. His next mission in life, he told Gerard, was to redeem the souls of the drunken and wanton Marble Bar miners and lead them all into the house of the Lord. Suddenly, perhaps touched by the Saviour's spirit, the

Reverend leapt to his feet, spread his arms wide and insisted Gerard join him in prayer. Gerard declined this invitation, preferring instead to gaze out the window at a vast treeless plain of red dirt and hot rocks baking beneath a hellion sun.

Occasionally, Gerard saw kangaroos bounding along beside the train as it rattled along the iron tracks. Having never seen such a sight, he thought that this was definitely something his city readers would love to read about. Out on the horizon, emus – the flightless birds without a brain amongst the mob – with feathery bodies supported on stilt-like legs would streak military fashion along. When the bird in front stopped, it would lead the mob in a wide circle, stirring up a willy-willy of red dust.

Up front, the engine driver Cec had also seen the emus and was keeping a strict government eye on them. Having cleaned up quite a few of them from the tracks during his career, he didn't want to be rolling into Marble Bar Station with the front of his engine bedecked with feathers and bits of emu; especially not today, because today was the day that when he handed in his peaked cap and red bandana to the Stationmaster before he was officially retired.

Throughout his life, Cec had been a staunch railway man, but from now on, he was looking forward to dedicating the latter part of his life to his wife Mary and getting to know those grandkids of his, of which he had eight.

Keeping his eyes focused on the shiny metal tracks ahead, he began to daydream of these days to come. While Cec daydreamed, Dobson was hurrying along the embankment of a dry creek bed, one that had not seen a spit of water for years. With his eyes fixed north, he was watching out for the first spiral of smoke that would herald the coming of the train.

Directly ahead, it was not smoke that Dobson first saw, but a young man feverishly trying to dig out a spring cart that had bogged in the soft sand. It was one of those station Johnnies, a name given to the Chinese houseboys who worked on the stations whose bosses were too mean to pay a white man's wage.

Dobson recognised the cart as belonging to Sam McIntyre, a mean-spirited man who owned a cattle station no less than 5 miles away. Having heard it straight from the station cook's gob, Dobson knew that every week McIntyre would send one of his Johnnies to town to pick up station supplies, including the mail and six bottles of fine Scotch whisky. Dobson, with a lick of his lips, decided that a man really should give this poor little bastard a hand to dig the cart out. But before he did that, he scanned around, noting that there was no sign of the nag that pulled the cart.

"Probably bolted for home," he muttered to himself. Thus far, there was no sign of any red dust that would indicate an approaching search party, which normally would be sent out after a horse had galloped home minus the cart. Dobson rubbed his hands greedily, then stepped out of the bush.

"Oi, Johnny Wong," he called, "Got yerself bogged, I see."

The young Johnny stopped his digging, stood up and looked suspiciously at the old swaggy before him. He had been told by the boss often enough not to trust any of this type of bludger out on the track, especially any swagmen.

"Ay lad, you remember me?" asked Dobson, "Your boss, him friend to me. He sent me to look for you. Wants to know where his flamin' cart is."

The Johnny squawked like a cockatoo, "Bossie angry?"

Dobson leered, then made a scissor action with two fingers. "Boss say he gonna cut your balls off if you break his cart."

The Johnny yelped like a wounded cattle dog, then fled, hurtling over the low-lying scrub with his long plaited qui flying out behind him. Dobson chortled as he turned with a mischievous grin towards the abandoned cart.

Back on the train, Cec was miffed to see that someone had hung the "Go Slow" flag from outside the railway siding. Nobody had said anything to him about any maintenance work going on along the track today. He toed young Alex, who was napping on the floor in between shovelling coal. Alex scrambled to his feet "What? We already there, Cec?"

Cec grunted, "Nah. A few more miles yet." Then he quizzed, "Hey, did anyone from the office or the yard tell ya about any track work goin' on today?"

"Nah, Cec. No bugger said nothin' to me. Why?"

"Well, 'cause some coot has hung out the 'Go Slow' flag. That's why. Maybe it's them larrikins from Wondy Station again. If it is, and I get my hands on them little blighters, I'll wring their scrawny little necks."

Alex punched a fist into his other hand.

"Yeah, Cec, that'd be real good, but just in case it ain't, how 'bout I keep a look out, and you watch the line from the side?"

"I see you're gonna make a fine railway man, young Alex," said Cec, as he squeezed the upper half of his body out of the cabin.

Alex remained vigilant. His eyes never left the track, and as the train rattled along the line and around the bend, he could see something lying on the rails. It looked like a man. He wrenched the emergency break down hard. The metal wheels of the train locked with a deafening squeal, sparks flew, and passengers screamed, many sent sprawling from their seats out into the aisle, and Cec was nearly flung out onto the tracks.

"Bloody strewth, Alex!" Cec roared, as he pulled himself back into the cabin. "Why did you go and do a fool arse thing like that? You know I am the only one allowed to touch that emergency brake!"

"Cec, look!" Alex pointed with a shaking finger ahead. His voice pitched a few octaves higher. "There's a bloody bloke lyin' on the track, and he ain't moving. I betcha he's bloody dead."

"I think ya maybe right, son," Cec replied, grumbling to himself as he slowly climbed down the ladder. "Last day on the job, and I have a bloody stiff to deal with."

Along the length of the train, passengers began popping their heads out of the windows. In a mixture of panic and confusion, they demanded to know, "What's happened? Have we crashed?"

Cec spun around. He raised his hand and shouted, "Pass the message along. All passengers must stay onboard. No one is to leave the train, and that is a government order."

Meanwhile, Alex – remembering the golden railway rule about not alarming passengers unduly – reassured them, "Nothing to worry about, folks. Just a dead body on the track. We'll get it shifted quick smart, and then we'll be back on our way again."

Sensing his first big scoop, Gerard ignored the government order and jumped from the train. With pencil and pad in hand, he ran to where Cec and Alex stood looking down at a man who – as it turned out – wasn't dead. More in repose. His face was covered with a battered felt hat, and his swag lay strewn across the track. Boots pointing midday showed a man who knew how to cobble his own boots with crumpled old newspaper pieces poking out through the soles.

Cec gave Alex a nudge. "You know this 'ere fella ?"

"Which one?" replied Alex, his head turning around. "The dead bloke, or this bloke 'ere sketchin' the scene?"

Cec placed his hands on his hips. "I'll worry about the dead one later." He thrust his chin out indicating Gerard. "Him. You know him?"

Alex eyed Gerard up and down, but in a friendly sort of way. "Never seen him before in me life, Cec, but he looks important."

Gerard responded by tucking his pencil up behind his ear. "Oh, I do apologise. I am Gerard Ward, a senior reporter for the *Fremantle Gazette*." He looked directly at Cec. "And you are?" he asked, removing the pencil and licking the lead.

Cec threw his arms in the air. "That's all I flamin' need on me last day with the railways – a bloody dead body, and a nosey parker bloody reporter from a newspaper, and me train runnin' late on me last day."

Cec glared down at the body on the track. "Take his hat off, Alex, and let's see what we have."

Alex dropped to his knees and removed the hat. Staring down in disbelief at the face, he exclaimed, "Bloody strewth, it's that flamin' Swagman Dobson!"

Cec's face mottled purple. His blood pressure skyrocketed, as did his hard leather boot as it aimed for Dobson's head, but seeing the horrified look on the reporter's face, he dropped his foot and scuffed the hard red baked dirt instead. Turning sharply, he strode back to the train, with Alex close by his heel.

Gerard ran after them, calling, "Excuse me, but you can't leave this man on the line. He is obviously terribly intoxicated."

"More the pity!" bellowed Cec, as he climbed the ladder of the driver's cabin. "That way, the little cockroach won't feel it when I run over him with me train."

Dobson, who had been foxing all along, shot up onto his feet. Clamping his hat on his head, he shouted, "Aw, c'mon, Cec. It was just a joke. It's me war wound, Cec. I can't walk that far. I only need a ride to The Bar, mate."

So it was that the train pulled into Marble Bar Station late. Carrying his Gladstone bag, Gerard lugged it up the main street looking for the Iron Clad Hotel.

The hotel, located in the middle of the main street, was easy to find, and when Gerard presented himself in the front bar, the barman told him he needed to check in with the housekeeper. She could probably be found somewhere in the back of the hotel. "Try the laundry first?" he suggested.

He found the housekeeper sweltering over a copper of boiling sheets.

"Excuse me," he said, tapping on the open door. "I'm Gerard Ward. My newspaper has made arrangements for me to lodge here."

"You're late," she snapped back, not turning her head.

Gerard was taken back by her curt manner. Changing hands with his leather Gladstone bag, he replied tight lipped, "I can hardly help that. The train was unavoidable delayed by a——"

She tossed a lump of blue dye into the boiling copper.

"Not good enough" she rebuked him. Shaking her hands dry, she removed a key from a bunch that hung from around her waist, holding it up. It was an invitation for Gerard to take it, but when he tried to do so, she snatched it back.

"Not so fast, laddie! There's some rules you need to know first." She raised a hand with her fingers outspread began ticking them off, one by one. "There'll be no women in your room, no spewing or pissing over the veranda, and if you spoil me sheets, you'll be washin' em yerself. Breakfast is at seven, no sooner, no later, on the dot. Same with lunch at twelve noon, and supper at seven. On Sundays, you fend for yerself."

Gerard assured her that he would be the model house guest, and as she led him up the back stairs and along the corridor, she said, "My name is Elizabeth, and that there is the bathroom. You'll find a bucket in there."

She brusquely added, "And I don't take kindly to anyone emptying the pisspot over the veranda rail."

"I'll try to remember that," said Gerard, keeping a straight face.

Finally, they stopped outside a closed door. Inserting the key, she unlocked it, handed it to him and without another word bustled off back down the corridor.

When Gerard stepped inside the room, the smell of bee's wax polish rose to greet him. The room was spotlessly clean, with a single bed, a wardrobe and a dresser. On a small table beside the bed stood a glass and a water jug that was covered by a beaded net doily. Placing his bag on the floor, he peered under the bed. Yes, there it was, the chamber pot. A set of double doors led out onto the veranda. He opened them and walked outside. Directly by the door was a chair. A little rickety, he thought, but good enough to sit and watch the sun go down on some evenings.

He took two steps to the edge of the veranda and looked over the railings to a town of rust-coated corrugated roofs and gnarled trees. Hearing gruff voices and what sounded like a howl of protest, he leaned over the railing to see what the commotion was all about. There was Dobson, being frogmarched across the street by the local constabulary in a not so gentle fashion.

"Why, it's that dreadful old man!" Gerard said to himself. He curbed the urge to call out, "Good job, Sergeant." Instead, he returned to his room and began unpacking his bag, first selecting a fresh change of clothes, then stowing the bag on top of the wardrobe. He headed to the bathroom to wash and change. After all, he didn't want to be late for dinner on his first night, and the thought of a public berating from the housekeeper Elizabeth terrified him.

Dinner was a set menu of three slices of fatty cold mutton, a sad limp salad and a hard-boiled egg, followed by a piece of apricot pie with thin, runny custard. Asking for a fresh pot of tea, Gerard was curtly told by Elizabeth, "The kitchen is closed."

He decided that good manners was better than going head to head in a verbal battle with Elizabeth and remained quiet. Thanking her for a wonderful meal, he rose and went into the bar area for a drink. Anything, he thought, to eradicate the taste of that disgusting mutton.

Chapter 2

The bar was packed with noisy, dusty-faced miners. The smell of their sweat, from hard yakka down in the pit, layered the room and made Gerard feel acutely embarrassed by his cleanly scrubbed face and clean clothes. He edged his way to the bar and sat down on a stool, only to be told by a nearby drinker, "Oi mate. Yer can't park yer arse there! That's Dobson's stool. He'll have a piece of ya when he comes in if he catches ya sittin there."

A portly man within the group shouted, "Oh, let the city slicker park his bum there. Dobson's been pinched again, so we won't be seeing him in 'ere tonight."

Another in the group of drinkers who was known as The Punter shouted back, "What the blazes has he been nicked for this time?"

The portly man guffawed, "For stoppin the bloody train this arvo, and Cec, well, he's fit to be tried, tellin' the beak at the courthouse that stoppin' a government train should be a hangin' offence."

This news had The Punter circulating and whispering

furtively behind his hand to the other drinkers.

Gerard, tired from his long journey and the events of the day, was not very interested in this bar room gossip, and seeing that the barman was busy, he sat looking at the array of dusty spirit bottles that sat haphazardly along the top shelf. Below that, oblique glass mugs were lined up in a more orderly fashion. On the bottom shelf were lumps of iron ore that served as paper weights for the bar tabs, not that they would flutter away from the wind that could barely be felt from the slow thumping ceiling fan as it slowly turned above.

Finally, it was Gerard's turn to be served.

"Well mate, whaddaya havin'?" asked the harried barman. Gerard ordered a small glass of ale.

"Perhaps bloody not, mate. I don't serve small ales in 'ere,'" was the reply.

"Well then, I shall have an ale in whatever fashion you choose to serve. That will be fine by me," Gerard replied.

"Good," said the barman, reaching for a glass mug, and in a more pleasant tone added, "My names Blackie. Me and me sister Lizzie run this pub. Now that'll be a bob, mate. And the rule round 'ere is, you leave ya money on the bar. I got no time to be hangin' around waitin' while you dig in ya pants for coin."

Opening his wallet, Gerard extracted a pound note, then emptied his pockets of coin, of which Blackie fingered one.

"Ain't you the new newspaper bloke that helped

Dobson?" he asked.

"I wouldn't say that I was much of a help, exactly," remarked Gerard, sipping the frothy head of his first North West Ale. "And my name's Gerard," he said, then added from years of habit, "Gerard Ward. *Fremantle Gazette*."

Resting an elbow on the bar top, Blackie ignored the drinker who shouted, "Oi Blackie, me bloody glass is empty. Whaddya doin'? Havin a smoke up there?"

Blackie hollered back, "Go piss on it, Charlie! Can't ya see I'm chattin' to the new bloke 'ere. Showin' him some country hospitality."

Still holding Gerard's coin, Blackie rolled it up his hand, balanced it expertly between his thumb and forefinger, then flicked it high into the air. It spun a number of times then landed back on the bar.

"Tails it is, lads," he shouted, then dropped the coin back into Gerard's pile. "Keep your bob. This drink's on me, mate," he said with a friendly wink.

No sooner had Gerard finished his ale than Blackie was back with a refill. Again, he settled in for another of his little chats, the subject of course being Dobson.

Casually, Blackie picked his teeth with a matchstick. "Dobson's a bit of a legend around 'ere," he said. "And when he's in town, we all keep a lookout for him." He called out to the bar: "Ain't that right, fellas?"

A few "too rights" were heard, amidst murmurs of assent and raised glasses.

Blackie scratched the side of his nose and added,

"They're sayin' Dobson's now lookin' at a month in the slammer. Time like that will kill the poor old bastard."

"So?" Gerard said abruptly. "What do you want me to do about it? Bail him out!"

"Well, now that you brought the subject up, Jerry," Blackie said.

"It's Gerard, not Jerry," corrected Gerard. "My name is Gerard."

"Oh yeah, that's right. I'll try to remember that," said Blackie with a grin. "Now, about Dobson. Heart of gold he has, and me and the boys, well, we'd like to bail the poor bastard out, but none of us can raise a cracker. Me pubs just about bankrupt, and the boys 'ere aren't paid for another month."

"Well, that's a bit of bad luck for this Dobson fellow, then," said Gerard, who had an inkling what was about to come next.

Blackie cleared his throat. "The boys and me were thinkin', umm, that maybe your newspaper would come to the party and help old mate out. It's only five quid, and we reckon your newspaper can easily afford that."

Gerard bent his elbow and rested his chin on his hand. "Hmm, five pounds, you say? That's a lot of money to justify to my editor." He pursed his lips, then gave an apologetic look. "I doubt that he will agree to that."

Blackie yawned in a bored manner, not once but three times. "That's ok," he said. "We'll ask the *Hedland Miner*.

That's a rag up in Port Hedland. They done a lot for this town. You know, town spirit sorta thing. Gotta say, it ain't gonna look good for your mob when the town hears that your newspaper done refused to help poor old Dobson."

Gerard cocked an eyebrow as Blackie drummed his fingers on the bartop. "Look Jerry, I really like you, so be a shame to see your newspaper go down the gurgler in these parts, but I reckon…" Blackie moved in closer. "What about a Swagman of note, so to speak, and he could tell you a few yarns that would curl your whiskers."

Gerard slapped his hand on the bar. "That's an interesting thought, and putting it like that Blackie, I think my editor may just agree." He held his hand out to seal the deal, and Blackie held his out for the fiver.

Removing a five-pound note from his wallet, Blackie snatched it and held it high.

"Hey, Claude." he shouted. "Take this ere fiver over to the nick and bail old Dobson out, will ya. Be quick about it and get back 'ere quick smart too."

Gerard waited over an hour for Dobson to arrive and was beginning to think that maybe he should call Blackie to task when a disturbance behind him made him turn around. Dobson, standing in the doorway with the heavy hand of the law on his shoulder, looked dour, but the sergeant was grinning from ear to ear as he pushed him forward, telling the throng of drinkers, "I believe he's all yours."

Dropping his swag, Dobson looked meanly around.

"Where's the geezer who put up me bail?" he growled.

Immediately, the finger was pointed towards Gerard, and Dobson, with spittle forming at the side of his mouth, roared, "Who told you to go stickin ya nose in me business?"

As to be expected, Gerard was astonished at his lack of gratitude. "Is that the way to speak to a man that has just saved your life?" said Gerard. "Anyway, Blackie said you'd die in jail if I didn't bail you out."

"If Blackie told yer to stick a branch up ya arse, would you do that too?"

"Most definitely not," retorted Gerard. "I am not that much of a fool."

"We'll see about that." Dobson's eyes swivelled around the bar. "Who's doin' the bettin' then?"

Someone called out it was The Punter. "He's payin' three bob against the toff 'ere bailin' ya out."

Dobson leered. "Reckon they made ya look like a right Billy Muggins then," he told Gerard. "You got conned out of five quid, and me, I'm out of five days grub and a bed to boot."

"Five days!" exclaimed Gerard, pinning Blackie a stern look. "You said he'd be locked up for a month."

Blackie, standing nearby, looked sheepish. "Well, that's right, but by the time he finishes stirrin' up the beak, he'll end up doing a month, or more."

"Yeah," hooted Dobson. "And ya plum done me outta free board for a month. The wet season startin' soon. Gonna be pissin' down with rain, and where do you think I'm gonna sleep?'

"Definitely not with me," said Gerard

"Aah, get yer Nancy arse off me bar stool. I need to do me sums to work out how much yer owe me."

Gerard picked up his ale. "I beg your pardon. Did I hear correctly? Did you imply I owe you money?"

"Yep. And if yer didn't, then yer better get them spuds washed outta yer ears," Dobson said as he peered closer to Gerard. "Oi! Don't I know your ugly mug from somewhere?"

"We had the pleasure earlier," Gerard said rather piously. "I saved you from being run over by a train."

"So now yer think you're me bloody guardian angel, do ya?"

"I doubt the Devil would want that job," Gerard said.

Dragging a stool across, Dobson plonked himself down and sat shoulder to shoulder with Gerard at the bar. Seeing Elizabeth come behind the bar, he cupped his hands and shouted, "Hey sourpuss, get your fanny over 'ere and pour me an ale."

When Elizabeth delivered the drinks, Dobson nodded to Gerard's money. "Cut it outta there. And don't fiddle me change."

Gerard's brows shot up. He looked at Elizabeth. "Why am I buying his drinks?" he asked.

Elizabeth replied with a pithy look. "Well, you' re the silly sod who bailed him out. More fool you are."

Picking up the pound note, she rang it up in the till and placed the change back down on the bar. Dobson's grubby hand shot out to cover the money.

"You're twenty-nine quid short!" he said to Gerard. "A quid a day it is to keep me locked up."

Gerard hammered his fist on the bar. "Dobson, I owe you nothing! In fact, you owe me five pounds, and the only way I will see that again is by taking you straight back to the jail."

"Yer can't do that." smirked Dobson "You think the sarge will want me back smellin' up his cells and makin' trouble? He's no Billy Muggins. He got it writ down that ya bring me back for thirty days, or I get meself in trouble, then we both in the slammer sharin' the same cell."

Chapter 3

Dobson spent the night camped out beside the old rainwater tank, out the back of the Iron Clad Hotel. He lay awake, thinking about the events of the day. Some of the lads from McIntyre's station who came into the pub for a late night's drink, before heading back to their mustering camp, had let on that McIntyre himself was coming to town come morning, to have him charged for pinchin' his booze off the cart.

"Damn little Johnny Wong," he muttered as he looked up at the stars.

As luck would have it, McIntyre was married to the sarge's sister, and it was a cert that they'd be locking him up. Not that being locked up ever bothered him that much, and it wasn't everyday a Billy Muggins like that Gerard bloke comes along.

"Aw shit!" Dobson muttered, then lifted his hat and scratched his head. He wasn't about to give up thirty days of free grog for nothing. He needed a plan that would get that bleedin' newspaper bloke outta town for a while.

Gerard had slept well, waking only when Dobson placed a kerosene lamp on the bedside table next to him.

"C'mon, shake a leg," said Dobson "Yer wanna know me story, then I'll tell it to yer, and ya can write it along the track. Now we gotta get goin'."

"What's your damn hurry, Dobson?" asked Gerard, sitting up and pulling the bedsheets aside.

"Me mates waitin', that's me hurry."

Gerard got out of bed and stretched. "I don't think so. Look outside, it is hardly daylight."

"On me honour, me mate's waitin' for us." Dobson looked slyly. "Ya 'ave to come along on account yer the Billy Muggins responsible if a bloke gets himself into trouble."

"Oh, blast you, Dobson!" said Gerard, annoyed as he pulled the chamber pot from under his bed. He padded to the bathroom with Dobson close behind. At the door, he stopped. "If it's ok with you, Dobson, I really do need to take a pee, and that is something I like to do in private."

"Why don't ya just piss over the veranda like the rest of us do?" Dobson remarked, giving the rose-patterned chamber pot a scathing look.

"Oh, for heaven's sake!" said Gerard. He opened the bathroom door and hurriedly locked it behind him.

"Hurry up in there," called Dobson through the door. "I forgot to tell ya, I already woke sourpuss up and told her to get yer breakfast ready. She'll be right pissed if yer late."

"Well, thank you Dobson," came Gerard's sarcastic reply. "That was indeed exceedingly thoughtful of you."

Placing the kerosene lamp on the floor, Dobson called again, "I'll leave the lamp 'ere. Don't want ya breakin' your fool neck comin' down the back stairs. When ya had yer feed, I'll be waitin' out the front of the pub for ya."

Gerard lingered over breakfast, and when he thought he had kept Dobson waiting long enough, he left the dining room and sauntered off to the front on the hotel, where Dobson waited with his swag at his feet.

"Should I pack a bag?" asked Gerard, but Dobson just shook his head. "I got everything we need, and we ain't goin' far."

The heat of the morning sun was breaking ground when they left town, and a few miles on, Gerard called a halt. "We have to stop, Dobson, it's too damn hot to walk," he said, pointing to a stringy bark tree. "Why not sit over there for a rest?"

"You can, but I gotta keep goin'," Dobson said.

"Blast that old man!" cursed Gerard, as he doggedly followed on, and though it was hard going keeping up with this man thirty years his senior, Gerard was determined to do so.

It wasn't long before he collapsed in screaming agony. The heat and sweat caused a mass of stinging blisters between Gerard's thighs, bum and testicles. He howled in pain as he kicked and tugged his trousers off.

Dobson threw his swag to the ground. "You're just a bloody Nancy," he declared, as he hunted in his bag for a bottle of salve. He tossed it to Gerard. "Rub this on your arse. You'll be right in a day or two."

"I can't. It's far too painful to touch," moaned Gerard.

"Looks like I gotta do it for yer, then," said Dobson. "Stand up, legs apart and bend over."

When Gerard was in position, Dobson yelped, "Crikey, yer got bush fly maggots crawlin' up your arse!"

"I have what?" cried Gerard, mortified.

"Bush fly maggots. Just hang about a tic, I'll be right back," Dobson said. He returned whittling the end of a leafy branch. Plucking Gerard's handkerchief from his pants pocket, he tore it into thin strips, greased it with salve and then wound it around the end of the stick.

"This, mate, is a bush remedy for eggs up the arse. Gotta be quick, or you'll be shittin' maggots for a week."

With the skill of a bush rectal surgeon, Dobson inserted the stick up Gerard's rectum, and when he was done, he gave Gerard a bit of a slap on the bum. This had him standing up smartly.

"Now what?" asked Gerard, smarting at the burning pain.

"We keep movin', that's what," said Dobson, as he tucked the salve away in his swag. Dobson walked off with a bounce in his step while Gerard, looking remarkably like a bush turkey with a leaf protruding out, followed at a much slower pace.

Further down the track, Dobson was waiting under a tree, and when he saw Gerard, he lifted his hat, fanned his face and called out, "You can get rid of that stick now, recon' all of them maggots be gone by now." And Dobson broke into a fit of hilarity.

"What's so fucking funny?" Gerard shouted, squatting to remove the stick.

Dobson choked back his laughter. "Remember back at the pub? What did ya tell me when I asked yer if someone told you to put a stick up your arse?"

Realising his own stupidity, Gerard shouted, "You're a blasted fiend of a man!"

He flung the greasy stick at Dobson.

As they carried on, Dobson's peals of laughter could be heard echoing around the bush. When they reached the Oakover River to camp for the night, Gerard again folded at the knees, this time lapsing into an inky pool of nothingness, which is just what Dobson wanted anyway.

Leaving Gerard, Dobson went into the bush in search of berries and plants that he ground together and put in the billy to boil. While he waited for the brew to heat up, he forced water between Gerard's cracked lips. When the mixture from the billy had thickened and cooled, he rolled Gerard over and plastered it over the weeping blisters.

Evening came, and Dobson bided his time by whittling wood. When he heard a familiar cooee calling from the bush, he quickly came to his feet, but before leaving, he stamped out the campfire, just in case that Billy Muggins rolled over and into it while he slept.

Dobson joined his friends, daubed with white clay in a nearby clearing. Around a small campfire, they sat in a circle and spoke – in a lingo that only a very few white men would understand – of things past and things yet to come. At sunrise, Dobson left them and returned to camp.

When Gerard woke that morning, he was surprised to find he felt little pain, considering the condition he had been in yesterday. Tentatively, he reached around and felt his backside. The blisters were now hard calluses. He came to his feet, but a wave of nausea and dizziness had him bending over. He waited for it to pass, then walked slowly to the bushes to urinate, where he passed a bloody stream of urine.

He aired his concerns to Dobson, but Dobson just shrugged. "Happens a lot when a bloke first comes bush. Yer kidneys take a bit of a hammerin', but like your arse, they'll toughen up in a day or so. Now, if you don't mind," he said, pulling his felt hat down over his eyes, "I been watchin' over ya all bloody night, and I need to get a bit of shuteye in 'fore we move on."

Gerard was not as blasé about his kidneys as Dobson was. He knew he needed plenty of water to flush them out. Picking up the billy, he walked to the water's edge.

Hearing Gerard's footfall, Dobson peered out from under the brim of his hat. "Whadda yer doin now?" he shouted.

Gerard, standing knee deep in the water, held up the billy. "I have to flush my kidneys out, so I'm getting water to boil up.

Dobson sat up and shouted: "Forgot to tell ya! That water is poison, mate. They dump all the shit from the mine sites in there. Only water fit to drink round 'ere is me piss, and I don't think ya fancy that."

Was this God's retribution to him for not joining the good Reverend Stoner in prayer, thought Gerard, as he eyed the water thirstily.

Grudgingly, Dobson got to his feet and swung his swag up. "Well, ya comin'?" he shouted, "or ya just hangin' around there waitin' for the church picnic to come along?"

"To where?" asked Gerard, staggering up the embankment. "Back to Marble Bar?"

Snatching the billy back, Dobson tied it to his swag. "Yeah, and that's a day's walk from 'ere. Doubt you'll be making it back there alive, mate."

Gerard could feel himself crumbling. He moaned his misery. "I can't walk another mile. I'm sick! There's blood in my urine, and I haven't passed my morning motion yet."

Dobson swore under his breath. He gave Gerard a shove. "Yer gettin' to be a pain in the arse, and ya should know all about that! Stop your blasted whingin', or I'll leave yer behind as tucker for the dingos."

That made Gerard's Adam's apple bob up and down. Dobson pointed up the track. "We ain't got that far to walk to hitch a ride. Reckon yer can make it that far, Nancy?"

Gerard wearily trudged on and was relieved when they left the bush track and ventured onto a wider road, with evidence of local traffic by the rutted tracks left by the cartwheels. Off to the side of the road was a large boulder. Dobson handed his swag to Gerard. "You. Sit over there. And don't ya move, no matter what," he ordered.

Gerard sat, miserably nursing Dobson's swag, while Dobson sat by the side of the track, leaping up only when he heard the jangling sounds of approaching horses in harness.

The Teamster spotted Dobson waving. He brought his foot down hard on the wooden brake, then stood up on the running board, reining frantically for the horses to pull up. The lead horses fought their bits and reared up, which caused a skirmish for the horses behind, but they stopped – with clouds of red dust swirling around – just a few feet short of Dobson.

When the dust began to settle, the Teamster roared his anger: "Yer stupid bloody fool! What yer tryin' to do, kill us all?"

Dobson shouted back, "Hang on, Joseph. It's me, Dobson."

Faster than the horses could change feet, the Teamster's tone changed, and he smiled. "Well, well, well… Whatta yer know, then? If it ain't the Swagman 'imself. Shoulda bloody known it was you. How ya goin', mate? Been some time since I last seen ya around."

Hearing the exchange of words, Gerard's head snapped up. Dobson had just about killed the lot of them, and all this Joseph could say was, "How ya goin mate?"

"Much bleedin' better since I cast me mince pies on you, me old mate," replied Dobson beaming. "Now Joe, ya goin' anywhere close to Dawson's Pub?"

"Well, no, but I reckon I can make a detour. Hop on up, Dobson. Who's yer mate?" he asked, seeing Gerard sitting with his head buried in his hands.

"Can ya bring 'im along as well?" asked Dobson. "The fella's sickenin' real bad."

Joseph was reluctant: "Yer know the bosses rules 'bout me pickin' up strangers. Oh heck! Okay. Just chuck the bugger up the back."

With Dobson perched up front beside Joseph and Gerard wedged in the back of the cart between a barrel and a bag of spuds, they set off. Gerard swore that when they reached wherever they were going, he was going to find a lock-up and hand Dobson back in.

This man's story was just not worth it.

Chapter 4

The town of Dawkins squatted around a pub, a post office cum general store, harness and machinery sheds and an assortment of ramshackle out buildings. Set aside and down the track was the local cemetery that bedded the bodies of the prospectors that had staked claims in the 1890s.

Hot days and red dust made everything look perpetually tired and spiritless, including the tall, raw-boned woman dressed in a white blouse and long black skirt standing on the veranda of the Dawkins Pub. The woman, Kathleen, leaned against the rail and watched only half-interested as two bearded prospectors dismounted their horses and tied them to the hitching post in front. Being anti-social men, they did not greet her or even give her a polite nod but just brushed past and walked into the pub.

Running her hands through her red hair, Kathleen patted her bun back into shape, then turned her face upwards as rainbow-coloured parrots swooped and squabbled as they fought for roosting space in the only gum tree in Dawkins.

She loved the parrots. They added the only colour to her drab life of living and running the pub in this god-forsaken place. With a heavy-hearted sigh, she turned and walked slowly back into the front bar, where her husband Robert was serving customers, a handful at this time of the day, but this would change she hoped when the mine knocked off.

What customers there were sat hunched over silently drinking and were so unlike the ribald skylarking drinkers from the Ironclad. Sitting alone at the furthest end of the bar was a miner known only by his nickname, "The Poet."

"Mad as a two bob watch" is how Robert described him, because The Poet only spoke to one man, and that was his friend Tobias – who had long since passed away – or to Kathleen. He had a habit of sprouting poetry at the oddest moments.

The Poet's glass was empty, so Robert swooped in. "Another one?" he asked.

"You want another ale, Tobias?" The Poet asked his invisible friend. Seeing Kathleen enter the bar, he pointed at her. "Look Tobias, it's Kathleen. Ain't she a pretty little thing today with those ribbons in her hair? What was that, Tobias? Yes, that's a good idea, Tobias. We'll give her a penny, and she can spend it at the lolly shop. She'll like that, Tobias. Won't you, our sweet Kathleen?"

"Like what?" asked Kathleen, coming to stand next to him to lay a hand on his shoulder.

"Tobias wants to give you a penny, dear. You can spend it at the lolly shop if you like."

"Why, thank you, Tobias," Kathleen pocketed the imaginary penny, playing along. "A lolly would be nice, but what I would like is to hear one of your poems."

"Did you hear that, Tobias? Kathleen wants to hear one of my poems," and The Poet began to chant.

"I've been a prisoner at Port Macquarie, Norfolk Island and Emu Plains.

Castle Hill and Toongabbie too.

I've worked in chains these three long years.

Beastly treated, legs in irons, my back they flogged, The cat of nine tails you know."

He finished with misty eyes before tears formed and rolled down his craggy face. As she always did, Kathleen softly patted his work worn hands for some moments then left.

Outside the pub, the afternoon silence was broken with the arrival of the Teamster to discharge its human cargo. Dobson walked around to the back of the cart complaining as he claimed his swag. "I'm bloody perishin' for a drink," he said to himself.

Gerard was left to battle his own way off the cart, clambering over boxes and barrels.

Thanking the Teamster for the ride, Gerard trailed into the hotel to find Dobson already perched up at the bar with two grimy fingers up, signalling to Robert for two ales.

"Long time no see, you old bugger," welcomed Robert, placing one frothy glass in front of Dobson and one in front of Gerard. Dobson shifted the second ale across.

"That's mine," he said, thumbing towards Gerard. "Don't know what he's having, but I'll be damned if he's drinkin' my grog."

"Who's paying, then?" asked Robert curtly, and lest it be Dobson, his hands reached out to take back the glasses, but he wasn't fast enough; Dobson spat in each glass.

"I'm paying," said Gerard tiredly, then ordered up another ale to be delivered.

When his glass arrived, Dobson gave a resounding burp, then handed back his two empty glasses. "And make the next one in a bucket, Robert. That lot barely hit the sides," he said, wiping his mouth with the back of his hand.

Gerard drank quickly, though in a more gentlemanly fashion. Robert lurked close by, because he knew from experience that after the third glass, drinkers slowed their pace. Except for Dobson, that was, who was a bottomless pit. When Robert delivered the next round of drinks, he rested his elbows on the bar, and his eyes were fixed on Gerard. He asked Dobson, "You going out to the Station?"

Dobson nodded. "Yeah, been some time since I caught up with Max and his missus. I know they like it when I drop by. Lets 'em know I'm still alive."

Gerard, his thirst quenched and conscious of smelling just like Dobson, interrupted, "Is there somewhere I can have a wash and a meal?"

"Sure thing, Mister," Robert replied affably. He ducked down behind the bar and came up with a scratchy towel and a bar of used soap. He pointed to a doorway. "If you wander out to there, you'll find the wash rooms, and the kitchen is right round the back. And that'll be sixpence for the towel and soap, mate."

Gerard tossed some notes on the bar. "This is for the drinks, towel and dinner and a bed for the night," he said, then added, "and should there be change left over after that, it comes to my pocket, not Dobson's!"

Change left over! Something Robert had grave doubts about, especially the way Dobson was guzzling down the drinks faster than he could fill them up.

Robert turned to Dobson, assuming he had met Gerard out on the track. "Where'd you find him? Never seen you travelling with no white bloke before."

Dobson pushed his empty glass forwards. "He's a reporter bloke. Got it in his thick head that he wants to write about me life."

This impressed Robert, who enthused, "Crikey! That'll make you famous and rich."

"No, it won't," sniffed Dobson shaking his empty glass under Robert's nose. "The bloke don't know I got no past, least one that I go rabbitin' on about, and me future ain't lookin' so good. So that leaves the here and now, and the here and now is fill me fuckin' glass up!'

Robert quickly took the glass, refilled it, then returned. "Make sure me hotel gets a mention in your story, won't you?"

Dobson began guzzling the next pint down. "It'll cost you," he said.

"A jug of Muscat do you?" offered Robert.

"You're on, then," replied Dobson, sealing the deal with a spit on a handshake.

In his search for the bathroom, Gerard made a few wrong turns but finally located it. On his travels down corridors, he could not resist but to have a sticky beak in some of the rooms. They were all the same, small closet-type rooms, linoleum covered floors, sparsely furnished with a trundle bed, mattress, dusty red sheets and a neatly folded grey blanket.

The bathroom was passable with a deep bathtub on cast iron legs. As Gerard soaped his body, the smell of carbolic rose from the second-hand bar of soap. Stepping out of the bathtub, the scratchy towel did little to mop up his wet body, so Gerard helped this process along by mopping up the excess water with his singlet. He detested the thought of having to wear the same smelly clothing, but he gave them a flap to shake the dust out. Looking into the fly-speckled mirror, he finger raked his wet hair into place with his fingers.

Satisfied he looked as good as he was going to get, he followed the wafting aroma of a stew that led him past the hotel vegetable garden. He stopped, then grinned as he read the hand-painted sign staked between the carrots and cabbages: "Do not piss in the vegetable patch."

He found the kitchen and peered through the fly

screen door to see a red-headed woman engrossed in kneading a large ball of damper bread. He tapped politely, and she looked up. Wiping her hands on her apron, she came to the door and asked pleasantly, "Can I help you?"

Gerard explained his predicament. "Robert, the man in the bar, said I may be able to get an early dinner. I've just spent the last 24 hours in the bush."

Kathleen, taking in his gaunt appearance, could well believe that before her stood a starving man. She nodded her acquiescence to an early supper. She waved him into the dining room.

"Sit down there, and I'll see what I can rustle up for you."

Taking a seat in the dining room, Gerard noticed the same fading linoleum used on the bedroom floors also covered the tables. Grouped on each table were salt and pepper shakers and bottles of homemade tomato sauce. Having read the sign in the veggie patch, he pushed the sauce to the side.

Kathleen soon appeared with a plate of steaming Irish stew and placed it down in front of him then left. Gerard ate with relish and no sooner had he mopped up the last bit of gravy with the bread, and she was back again.

"Pudding?" she asked as she whisked the plate away. "Rice pudding with peaches?"

"That sounds wonderful," replied Gerard. "Oh, I'm sorry, I haven't introduced myself. I'm Gerard Ward, a newspaper-man from Perth. I'm setting up an office in Marble Bar."

"And I'm Kathleen," she said. Placing a hand on her hip, she asked, "Hmm, a newspaper man, huh? What would bring a newspaper man to Dawkins?"

"While I'm waiting for the troops to arrive with the printing press, I'm filling in my time by writing a story about a most interesting character that calls himself the Swagman."

Her hand dropped from her hip, her face heightened with colour. "You mean that Irish bog Dobson! The best thing anyone could write about him is his obituary!"

She turned and strode out of the dining room.

"Obviously not a fan of Dobson's either," thought Gerard, as he waited for his pudding to arrive.

Chapter 5

When Gerard finished dinner, he thanked a huffy-looking Kathleen then returned to the bar. There were a few new faces, including a mousy-looking woman preparing the Tilly lamps by filling and cleaning wicks in readiness for the evening ahead. He noticed Dobson was still parked on the same stool and appeared in a glum mood.

Gerard hailed Robert for a glass of ale. "You should really go and get something to eat, Dobson. That Kathleen makes the best Irish stew."

"Probably 'cause she's an Irish bitch," replied Dobson, staring moodily into his beer.

Gerard raised an eyebrow. "That's odd, because she called you an Irish… Oh, it doesn't matter what she called you."

Dobson harrumphed. "I know what she calls me."

Robert arrived. "The missus dish you up a feed?" he asked, as he placed the glass of ale in front of Gerard.

"Yes, she did," Gerard patted his stomach. "Great cook."

"Then that'll be three bob," said Robert, taking it from the money left sitting on the bar, which wasn't much.

"Oi!" Dobson gave a shout, "that's me drinking money yer' squandering on food!"

Gerard looked stern. "You are an unprincipled bastard, Dobson!"

"Don't yer worry yerself 'bout me principles," grumbled Dobson. "I got some principles, yer know. Not many, but I got some."

"Which are?" queried Gerard, cocking a brow and running a finger around the rim of the glass.

Dobson pouted. "I can't think of any just now. Give a man some peace and keep your gob shut for a while."

Gerard was happy to comply, but Dobson fidgeted, turning often to look at the front door.

"Are you waiting for someone, Dobson?"

"Yeah. Me mate Tom Thumb."

"Strange name for a man," thought Gerard.

Then Robert came rushing up and spoke to Dobson with urgency. "Tom Thumb just pulled up. He'll be here in a minute, so don't ya go anywhere."

"That's him now," said Dobson, pointing to the biggest man Gerard had ever seen, with legs like tree trunks and shoulders so wide he had to turn sideways just to get through the door. When he walked, the floorboards groaned beneath his weight as he lumbered his way to the other end of the bar.

Another man followed him in, his eyes continually flinching from side to side. "They call him the weasel," whispered Dobson behind his hand.

"A name most fitting," thought Gerard.

The weasel sidled up to Dobson. "Tom Thumb wants to have a little chat with you," he said hoarsely.

"Stay here, big ears," Dobson told Gerard. "This is nothin' you want to know about."

Gerard ordered another beer, and as he drank, he tried to eavesdrop on the conversation going on at the end of the bar, but a rowdy group of jackaroos arriving put paid to that idea. Dressed similarly in long pants and checked shirts, the new arrivals called for bottles to be brought, and Gerard deduced it must be payday with cheques being handed across the bar to Robert. Shortly after, more men trailed into the bar after the mine knocked off work. Extra tables were carried in and set up, with decks of cards laid out in the centre. Gerard had no idea where they came from, but women began arriving, dressed in their finest and heavily scented, titillating and mingling with the men.

"Another drink, Gerard?" Robert exchanged Gerard's empty glass with a full one. He berated a man who jumped the bar and donned an apron. "You're half an hour late!"

The bar became so busy that it was difficult to find space to bend an elbow. Gerard looked around for Dobson, but there was no sign of him, nor of Tom Thumb. He shrugged. Another glass of ale was delivered, but this one tasted bitter.

"Probably from a new keg," thought Gerard, but moments later, his bowels grumbled alarmingly, and the room began to pitch and sway.

Those nearby thought him just another drunk as he lurched off his stool and stumbled for the door. He made it to the vegetable patch before his legs gave way and he vomited, spraying the carrots, cabbages and turnips with the evening's meal of Irish stew, peaches and ale. Then he passed out.

Kathleen had exchanged her drab daywear for a brightly coloured skirt, bunched up at the side with a bow, displayed a long leg in fishnet stockings. Her frilled blouse, laced half way up, showed her well-rounded bosoms, and her hair cascaded down around her face.

She almost tripped over The Poet sleeping on the floor.

"Come on, love," she said, giving him a gentle shake and helping him to his feet. "Time you got yourself home. This is not a place for you."

He grasped Kathleen's hand. "Where's Tobias?" he asked piteously.

She reassured as she guided him through the crowd and out the door, "He'll be along in a minute, but he said for you to go on home. He'll be there soon."

The Poet's donkey Bleeter, which always roamed at will searching for dry feed, was nipping at the horses hitched at the rails. Kathleen helped The Poet on. With a toss of its head, the donkey set off at a brisk trot to take her master home.

Kathleen watched and was soon joined by her friend Molly.

"Someone should do something about that old man. It's dangerous him living out there in the bush, especially around those old mine shafts," Kathleen said to Molly.

"It's that poor little Bleeter donkey I feel sorry for," replied Molly. "Every night walking back home in the dark and over that ridge. Bleeding dangerous it is. God knows we don't want him going over the side, like them others."

Kathleen shot Molly a concerned look.

"Don't you worry Kathy, my friends are always watching out for him,' said Molly. Linking arms, Molly gave a grimace. "We better be getting back inside before that rogue husband of yours comes looking for us."

Bleeter arrived home safely, but she was stressed and brayed mournfully for her master, who was draped over her neck but had died some miles back. From out of the nearby bush, shadowy figures came and gently lifted The Poet from the donkey's back. One led the donkey away, while the others carried The Poet into his shack. They did not stay long. Leaving at a run, they dived for cover into the bush as the shack exploded, bursting into a fireball.

Back at the Dawkins Pub, Kathleen was paying the girls their nightly earnings. "You could go home," she said, for most of the men, having had their way with them, were now grouped around the piano singing ribald songs.

She was about to leave herself until Robert came up from behind and roughly grabbed her arm. "You ain't finished yet," he snarled.

"One day, Robert, and let God be my witness," she hissed, only for Robert to cruelly pinch her arm. His breath was foul on her face. "The only thing God will be witnessing is you with yer legs spread servicing one of his little helpers. Now get going!"

He roughly pushed her forward. "That Reverend Stoner is waitin' for yer out back."

Chapter 6

Gerard slept the night in the vegetable patch. He awoke with the sun's ray burning his face. Squinting and turning his face away, he lay collecting his thoughts. He burped last night's dinner and sniffed his own vomit. Reaching around, he patted his back pocket. His wallet was still there, which meant Dobson had not passed by.

He crawled up onto his knees, then came to his feet and staggered off to the bathroom, but someone had absconded with the bathtub. He went in search of Kathleen. She was in the kitchen cracking eggs into an enamel bowl, and she grinned to see him standing at the door with a hangdog look.

"Ready for breakfast? I've cooked up a mountain of chops and liver. It's all warming in the stove," she said cheerily.

"Maybe later," mumbled Gerard, feeling greener than the cabbages he had just spent the night with. He cleared his throat.

"There's a bit of a problem in the bathroom," he said.

"Problem?" said Kathleen, looking barely surprised.

"There's no bath," replied Gerard. "Well, least not one that I can see."

Kathleen laughed lightly. "It'll be those station boys again. They often take it to use as a water trough for their horses."

"Um… so when do you expect it back?"

"About a week or so, maybe," she said. Then she suggested, "Better use the laundry. There's plenty of water there and soap as well. Rinse off with a bucket." She took up the rotary beater and gave it a practiced whir.

Laying the beater down, she gazed after him. For a man not from the bush, he had a strong physique and was very handsome, no doubt about that – blue eyes, strong jaw and sandy ringlets framed his face. He was very polite and clean, something she liked in her men, but they were rare in Dawkins. And she should know, having serviced most of them.

Kathleen resumed her work and was pouring cake batter into a tin when Gerard returned.

"I hope you don't mind," he said, "but I borrowed somebody's razor. I have washed and cleaned it and put it back where I found it."

Kathleen smiled. "That's ok. It's probably one of the boys that nicked the bath. Ready for some breakfast now?"

"Perhaps a cup of tea and some toast. Had a bit of a night last night, so I doubt I could handle much more."

"Slept well, did you?" asked Kathleen with a knowing smile, but seeing him blush, she shooed him off. "Go on, wait in the dining room, and I'll bring your cuppa to you soon."

Gerard was on his second cup of tea when Dobson came barging through the door.

"There yer bleedin' are! I was lookin' all over the goddamn place for yer. How come yer didn't sleep in ya bed?"

He scrunched an eye. "Oh, never mind," he blustered. "We gotta get going now."

"You want a cup of tea?" Gerard asked waving to the pot. "It's still hot."

"That bleedin' muck will kill ya," Dobson said, as he shot a look over his shoulder to the door. "Will ya hurry along? I got meself into a bit of bother last night, and I don't want you gettin' into no trouble about it."

"Me in trouble?" said Gerard, buttering his piece of toast. "Who would I be getting into trouble with?"

"Them Johnny Hoppers from Nullagine, that's who," Dobson ducked out the door, looked around then came back in. "They'll be 'ere soon enough askin' questions, and I got no answers to give yet."

Gerard bit into his toast. "Well, last night, I slept in the vegetable patch. The cabbages and carrots can verify that. So what dastardly deed could you have committed now?"

"Nothin', he done nothin' at all," sniped the Weasel, who flitted in the door. Clutching Dobson's arm, he spoke in a hoarse whisper. "Tom Thumb says he's got problems with his cart. Betta yer leave now. Make yer own way to the station."

Gerard started to think he was throwing a party when Kathleen came rushing in. By the looks of her red rimmed eyes, she had been weeping. She placed a brown paper bag on the table next to Gerard.

"You'll need this," she sniffed. "I've made you some sandwiches, and there's some apricot tart as well. God only knows when you'll get your next decent meal."

Gerard levered himself out of his chair and rested the palms of his hands flat on the table, looking around at his uninvited guests. His words were stern. "Unless someone tells me what is going on, I have no intention of going anywhere with anyone, especially with you, Dobson."

Dobson, the Weasel and Kathleen exchanged worried looks. Kathleen dropped her head and murmured, "Best you tell him, Da."

"Da!" Gerard looked aghast. "Is Kathleen your daughter then, Dobson?"

"Yeah," replied Dobson, dropping into a chair. "I forgot to mention that, but she ain't the dastardly deed. There was a fire last night, out at the ridge, and now they lookin' to pin it on me."

"Who's looking to blame you?" asked Gerard.

"Just someone."

"And who is this someone?"

"Just bloody someone! But The Poet is dead."

Kathleen immediately resumed a fresh bout of weeping, while the Weasel kept lookout by the door. Dobson kept his eyes on the table watching the ants trail out of the sugar bowl.

Gerard folded his arms. "Well, Dobson, are you responsible for The Poet's demise?"

Dobson gave a determined jut of his chin. "Last night, Tom Thumb and me had to get something for The Poet. Don't ya go askin' what for, 'cause The Poet don't want no bastard to know. When we got back to the pub, The Poet was gone, so Weasel and me, we borrowed a couple of spare horses hangin' out front of the pub and took a ride to The Poet's shack, but when we got there, he was already dead."

"And the fire?" asked Gerard. "Did you burn the shack?"

Kathleen was agitated and interrupted. "Da," she pleaded, "If Robert comes in here, it'll be a case of what for, for me."

"Then in that case, I'll need some clothes to travel with, and water. I'm not leaving here without water," said Gerard, having decided to go along with Dobson.

"Wait here," said Kathleen racing out the door.

She whipped around the hotel, raiding a few sleeping bodies of their shirts, pants and a pair of boots. From the storeroom, she added a mop handle, thin blanket and a water bottle, then returned to the kitchen and handed them to Dobson. Spreading the blanket out on the floor,

Dobson fashioned Gerard his own swag, then with a hurried goodbye, they left the hotel, skulking away like thieves in the night.

They kept to the bush, avoiding the main road and stopping only to check that they were not being followed. Dobson pointed north. "Three miles on," he said, "there's a beautiful little waterhole. We can rest up till it cools off. Maybe camp the night."

The beautiful little waterhole turned out to be a crater of clear water ringed by high rocks. There was evidence that kids played there, with long ropes suspended from overhanging branches of trees that bordered the waterhole.

Gerard, foot sore and weary, found a comfortable rock, sat down and tugged his boots off while Dobson set up camp.

With the billy on the boil, Gerard opened up the paper bag. He pulled out a wrapped sandwich, but finding it drowned in tomato sauce and remembering the vegetable patch, he offered it to Dobson, who gave him a quizzical look.

"I prefer damper and jam," said Dobson, only to find that the ants had gone crazy over the sweet treat, so he tossed his food into the bush.

Dobson slid down onto his back, plumped his swag into a pillow, pulled his hat over his eyes and feigned sleep, if only to avoid having to answer Gerard's questions.

Gerard used the opportunity to wash off the morning's dust and cool down. The water was cold, but once refreshed, he climbed up the bank and lay down on a boulder to rest.

"What the blazes are ya doin' now?" called Dobson.

"Drying off," called back Gerard.

Dobson thumbed to the sun. "Ya silly arse. Get outta the sun! At this time of the day, it'll fry yer brains."

Gerard left his rock and took shelter under one of the scrubby trees, which fringed the rocks. "That didn't bother you yesterday!" said Gerard, picking up some flat stones and skidding them across the waterhole. "Yesterday, you were happy to leave me for dead. Feed me to the dingoes, if I recollect."

"That was yesterday," replied Dobson with a yawn. "Then I remembered how I'm up a bob every day with Blackie for every day I keep ya alive out here."

"You and Blackie?" Gerard dropped the stones, then turned around. "Laying bets on my life? Now I've heard it all."

"Oi! It's not just me mate! The whole of Marble Bar is bettin' on yer not comin' back, and oh yeah, forgot to tell ya, we're camping 'ere for the night, but 'fore it gets dark, I want ya to go bush and get me some cow dung pats."

"I just ate lunch. I'm not hungry yet," replied Gerard touchily.

"We're not eaten' them, yer bloody wrong!" Dobson wiped his brow. "We gotta burn 'em, 'cause when them blasted mozzies come in at night, you will bloody know all about it! One nip from them little bastards, and you'll be sicker than a dog, and as yellow as his vomit."

"Where do I find these cowpats, then?" asked Gerard compliantly as he tugged his boots back on.

Dobson swept a hand around the surrounding bush. "Anyplace out there! They're all over the blasted place. And don't get lost, 'cause I ain't comin' lookin' for ya."

There weren't many cowpats to be found, and what there was would have to do, thought Gerard. He carried them at arm's length back to camp. There was no sign of Dobson, so he dropped the pats and waited for him to return.

Night came, and Dobson still had not come back. Gerard was getting worried. What would he do if a hungry dingo came into camp, or a snake? He shivered, then threw another cow pat on the fire. When Dobson did finally wander back, Gerard was beside himself and shouted, "Where the hell have you been? I have been worried sick out of my mind."

"Now ya think yer me mother, do ya?" replied Dobson. He held out a clay pot. "Yer want some tucker?"

Gerard peered into it. "What is this?' It looks like—"

"Bungarra," cut in Dobson, as he dipped his hand in and pulled out a charred claw from a bush lizard. "Have a taste. Bloody good tucker."

Gerard sniffed the claw. It smelt okay, so he bit into it. Blood spurted and oozed down his hand.

"It's still raw!" he shrieked, flinging the meat away. Dobson, knowing what may come next, flung himself sideways, as a wooden spear came pinging through the air, embedding itself in front of Gerard.

Gerard jumped back, shouting, "What the fuck is that?"

"A message from me friends," said Dobson coming to his feet. He scooped up the meat that had fallen from the clay pot and stuffed a piece into his mouth. "Start chewin'. I think me friends are a bit touchy 'bout yer not likin' their tucker. Especially as they took the trouble to catch the blighter and cook him up."

Dobson slapped him heartily on the back. "That's the way, Mister Billy Muggins."

That night, Gerard found it hard to sleep. The spear remained in the ground, and he jumped at every noise. Bush fowls rustling, distant screams of mating feral cats, howling dingoes and Dobson whistling through his teeth as he slept.

Chapter 7

When Sergeant Roberts and Constable Vernon walked into the Dawkins Pub, Robert was sweeping up shards of broken glass from the floor. The officers, newcomers to the district, had not yet made their acquaintance with the publican, but they were about to as they took seats at the bar.

Laying aside the broom, Robert walked around the bar, as the sergeant watched him closely, summing him up as being a bit of a slippery eel.

Refraining from the customary handshake, the sergeant spoke bluntly. "I am Sergeant Roberts, and this attending officer is Constable Vernon. We are from the Nullagine Police Station and making enquiries into an incident that happened out at Jaspers Ridge last night."

"Yes, I know," replied Robert passing a phoney smile. "I sent you the telegram when I heard somethin' fishy was going on. What can I say, Sarge? You got to know I run a respectable pub. No gambling, and no prostitution. You boys having a drink?"

He casually reached behind to collect two glasses. "On the house, of course." he added.

The sergeant looked flinty. "Are you attempting to bribe officers of the law with alcohol, Mr Dawkins? Perhaps it may have worked for you in the past, but let me assure you, such a suggestion will work against you in the future."

Robert slipped the glasses behind his back and edged them back on the shelf. "I wouldn't dream of doing such a thing, Sergeant!"

His eyes mirrored his dislike, because he didn't like this new breed of bloody coppers they were sending up from the city. Stand offish lot of bastards they were, not even accepting a drink on the house.

The sergeant harrumphed: "Well, just remember that, Mr Dawkins. Now, I have a busy day ahead of me. I have no time to waste. I want to know who frequented this establishment yesterday."

Robert stroked his chin. "Well, Harry from the battery drops in every morning nearly on opening time, and Tom Smithers from up the road, he does too. Hopalong, maybe twice a week, but then he's got a missus. There's Mick the mute—"

The sergeant raised his hand. "Perhaps, say from four o'clock onwards to closing time." He turned around to his constable. "Are you getting all this down, Vernon?"

"Yes, Sarge. Every word, Sarge. Just like the manual says."

The sergeant swung back to Robert. "Shall we have another go, Mister Dawkins? The names of the people drinking in this hotel last night."

Robert gave a shrug. "Place was quiet as a church mouse last night, Sarge, that is if we had a church, which we don't, because the closest one is in Port Hedland, and aside from a few of the local station boys comin' in for a quick nip or two, there was also that hobo."

The sergeant cracked his knuckles. "A hobo, you say. By chance is his name Dobson?"

"Yeah, maybe it was. He came in with another fella, and they sat right there," Robert pointed to a table. "Didn't stay long. Just sat there watching The Poet gabbling to his mate Tobias."

The sergeant drummed his fingers on the bar. "Read the list of names back again, Vernon."

Clearing his throat, the constable held his notebook out. "Well, I got Harry from the battery, Tom Smithers from up the road, Hopalong, the station boys, Mick the Mute, Dobson, Mr Poet, a hobo, Tobias, the Church Mouse and some fellow keeping tabs on the Poet." He flipped the page.

"Enough, Constable." The sergeant flicked his fingers. "Scratch the chappie Church Mouse off the list. He was in Port Hedland. And your good wife, Mr Dawkins, where was she last night?"

Robert mopped his brow with his lank hanky. "Well, last night, me darlin' Kathleen had one of her splittin' headaches, so I told her to lock up the kitchen early, put her feet up, and I'd be along with a nice cup of tea when I shut the pub."

"So, your wife was sick in bed?"

"Well, you could say that… in bed with her feet up."

"Hmm," muttered the Sergeant. "Now The Poet? What can you tell us about him?"

"Comes in here every day about four. Keeps to himself, most preferring only to chat with his mate Tobias."

The sergeant raised a craggy eyebrow. "And where can I find Mr Tobias? I'd like a word with him."

Robert leaned part way over the bar and pointed out the door. "You head about a mile up the road, and you'll find him bedded down there."

Vernon snapped. "Don't be impertinent, Mr Dawkins! That's the cemetery."

"Yeah, that's right! Where you think old Tobias would be when he's been dead these last two years?"

"That's not what you said!" Vernon flipped back pages. "Aah, here it is. You said Mr Dawkins, and I quote, 'Just sat watchin' The Poet gabbling to his mate Tobias.'"

"Yeah, but that don't mean he was here. Ya see, The Poet, he still thinks his mate is still alive. Bit touched in the head, you see." Robert looked to each of the officers in turn. "You sure you don't want that glass of… ahem… water now?'

The sergeant looked up. "I think that's all for today, Mr Dawkins. We'll be on our way. We still have a few people to talk to, but we'll be back."

Robert waived. "You're welcome any time, Sarge," he said. Then he thought, "Friggin' hell."

The officers made their way along the dusty street, stopping occasionally to introduce themselves and have a bit of a natter with a few of the people that were about. They chatted to one man in particular who told them, "Best you speak with Fred." He pointed them further along to a blacksmith shop. "He'll know 'cause all he does is sit out front measurin' up the townspeople."

Fred was also the town's undertaker, and his trade as a blacksmith came in handy when folks wanted fancy do-das added to their box. When the policemen walked in, he was hammering up a box. Seeing them, he laid down his hammer and picked up a long wooden ruler.

"Ain't you fellas a bit young to be gettin' measured up," he asked, chuckling at his own joke.

Vernon grinned and pointed to the half-finished coffin. "Who's this box for?"

Fred gave the box a pat. "Old Jimmy Griffith, but he won't be needin' it. No sir, not today. 'cause Old Jimmy, well, he's still kickin' alive, but now come Saturday, well, maybe things will have changed by then." Fred paused. "You fellas wantin' to order one? Or are you just passin' by for a bit of a chin wag?"

"Just dropping by for a bit of a chin wag," replied the sergeant in a tone far friendlier than he had used with Robert.

Fred cackled. "Well, just remember, I don't talk ill of the dead."

"You bury everyone in town?" asked the sergeant, looking around.

"Most. Not that I make much of a quid out of it. Most of the miners around 'ere are dirt poor when they check out."

"You'd know The Poet then?" enquired the sergeant.

"Sure do! Hard to forget a fella that gave his mate one of the finest sends offs this town ever seen."

"His mate Tobias?" asked the sergeant.

"Yeah, Tobias. Him dyin' really broke the old bastard up. I remember The Poet wanted a real fancy box."

Fred sighed in remembrance, though not for the passing of Tobias but of his own fine blacksmithing work he had done on the coffin.

Vernon continued chatting with the undertaker, while the sergeant took a stroll around. "You had a busy morning, then?" he asked as he handled a broken cart spoke.

"Yep. Tom Thumb and his sidekick Arnie did a spoke in. They're a couple of teamsters that bring in supplies for the pub," the undertaker said.

"So, they were in town last night, then? That's interesting indeed," said the sergeant.

"Yeah," said Fred, unaware of the gravity of his words. "Stayin' at the pub they were. And what a night that must have been!"

"Really?" Vernon raised his brow. "And why is that?"

"Every man and his dog must have been in there last night… and damn noisy it was too, with riders gallopin' off in the middle of the night."

"Oh really," said the two police officers.

Chapter 8

Sitting under a gum tree waiting for a ride to come along, Gerard was so thirsty, he doubted he could spit far enough to christen the bush lizard that scuttled over his boots.

They were heading to Kangaroo Downs Station. Gerard was looking forward to visiting a real true-blue cattle station. "Otherwise, I would be on the next ride back to Marble Bar," he thought, giving Dobson a pointed look. It seemed like a hundred years since he had left the comfort of that magnificent bed back in the civilised city world.

Their ride eventually came along, which was a rickety old horse drawn cart. When the driver stopped, he shouted, "Hurry along, Dobson, I'm already runnin' late. I can only take you as far as the turn off, then you'll have to walk the rest of the way."

"That'll do us, Pete," replied Dobson. They climbed aboard, and with a crack of the whip, the horse broke into a fast trot. It was a hell of a ride. The track was narrow and corrugated, and Gerard was amazed that the old cart even held together.

The driver dropped them off close to the station turn off, and as they walked, Gerard incessantly asked, "How much further?"

The answer was always the same. "Just around the next bend."

After a few more bends, Dobson pointed ahead, "Look, you can see the homestead from here."

The homestead was built from sandstone rock with verandas all round, and as Dobson and Gerard came up the path, a tall man with a red beard clad in moleskin pants stood on the front veranda watching them. He cast a cursory glance at the grubby and unshaven man Dobson had in tow with him and frowned in puzzlement. As long as he'd known Dobson, he had never brought anyone to the station. He always travelled alone, so perhaps this fellow was looking for work and had hitched a lift on the same cart. A little unkept, perhaps, but the fellow didn't look that down at heel to him.

Nevertheless, he asked Gerard, "Are you looking for work?"

Gerard, feeling self-conscious now of the plum pudding swag balanced on his shoulder, lowered it to the ground. He stepped forward and extended his hand. "No, sir. I'm travelling with Dobson. My name is Ward. Gerard Ward, and I'm a journalist from the *Fremantle Gazette*."

"Max Huntingdale," said Max, extending his hand. Remembering his manners, he ushered them up to the veranda. "I'll fetch us some drinks. Poor devils, you must be parched."

With accustomed familiarity, Dobson plonked himself down on a white wicker chair. Gerard, displaying a little more finesse, remained standing and looked down at his dirty clothes.

"Good God, man," said Max. "Don't worry about a bit of red dust. Just take a seat, and I'll be right back."

Gerard sat, back erect perched on the edge of the chair. He had not sat long when it was time to rise again, as a woman dressed in blue taffeta and French lace with a cameo clasped tightly at her throat carried a tray of drinks towards him.

"Gerard, I'd like you to meet my wife Jane." He gave a chuckle. "But we call her Lady Jane."

"Stay sitting, Gerard," she said in an upper-class English accent. "We rarely stand on ceremony out here." Seeing Dobson, she exclaimed, "Dobson! What a lovely surprise."

Turning a few shades of red, Dobson mumbled an excuse about "needin' to see the boys," then scampered off down the veranda stairs. Max laughed. "My Jane has that effect on most men. Sends them running, eventually. I'm the only silly blighter that hung around."

"Oh, do shush, Max," Jane said, as she placed a tray of drinks on the table. "I am so looking forward to hearing all about you… but not right now, you'll have to excuse me. I have a butt of beef cooling on the racks and some very hungry camp dogs at the kitchen door."

Max was most hospitable. "I hope you can stay around more than a few days, Gerard," he said, pouring and handing Gerard a drink. "It's rare occasion we have visitors at all. Most don't like roughing it out here."

"That's kind of you, Max, but if I overstay my welcome, please let me know. I won't be offended, not one bit," Gerard drank his tea, the hint of mint making it very refreshing.

"Tell me, Gerard," asked Max, as he packed his pipe. "What on earth are you doing wandering around out in this wilderness with an old reprobate like Dobson."

"Now, that's a long story, but short version is that I'm doing a story on him for my newspaper. Human interest, that kind of thing for the city readers. In the short time I have known him, I must say he has led me on a bit of a song and dance."

"Well, that's Dobson for you," remarked Max. "Though I imagine he would be hard to pin down."

"Who needs pinning down?" asked Jane bustling back.

"Dobson does, dear," replied Max. "Gerard is doing a story on him for the newspaper! Rather amazing, don't you think?"

Jane showed her surprise. "And he agreed to that? I don't believe it," she said, casting a critical eye over Gerard. "I've had my niece Scherie fill the bath for you, and there's a change of clothes for you as well. So, go on, off you go. You'll feel better after a nice bath," she said with a kind smile.

An hour later, Gerard, freshly bathed, returned to his host, Max, on the veranda and found him sitting with a large cheese platter on his lap.

"You're just in time, Gerard." Max picked up a biscuit and a wedge of cheese. "Try this. Jane makes it."

Gerard popped the biscuit into his mouth. "Very tasty," he said, reaching for another.

Max lifted the tray onto the table and waved to it. "Help yourself, Gerard. Jane makes excellent cheese. By the way, did you see her herd of goats in the South Paddock when you came in?"

"Honestly, no," replied Gerard, feeling guilty that he had not.

"Well, don't tell Jane that," Max lowered his voice. "Those goats are her pride and joy, and if you want to get the best cut of beef, then it would be wise to mention them. Especially Floppsy, she's the black and white one."

Sitting back, Max repacked his pipe and puffed contently, while Gerard looked around the garden. Flowering bougainvillea hanging in clay pots gave splashes of colour – mauve and pink – around the homestead.

A number of quaint rockeries were filled with a variety of cacti and native bush plants. Tall white gums with leafy green foliage gave shade where it was needed most.

Seeing Gerard's observations, Max remarked, "This station Kangaroo Downs has its own underground water supply. Makes us very self-sufficient. If you get a chance tomorrow, have a look at the vegetable gardens."

"I know a lot about vegetable gardens," murmured Gerrard. Then he asked, "I assume you have been here a long time."

"About thirty years," replied Max with a chuckle. "Back in those days, my brother and I were a bit wayward, and our father, fearing we would run off the rails, bought this land. He thought the land would make men of us, and that it did by jove, but he worked us hard. Dobson too."

"Dobson did a day's work!"

Max tapped the bulb of his pipe into a bowl. "Well, we all did, including Dobson's wife Libby. Young Elizabeth was born on this station, you know."

"Who was born here?" asked Jane, who had arrived to inform them that dinner was ready.

"Elizabeth, dear. I was talking about Elizabeth. I was telling Gerard about those early days."

"Before my time," remarked Jane, with a wink at Gerard. "One rarely gets a chance to show off," she said.

"So Scherie and I removed the dusters from the formal dining room. We are dining there tonight."

Max groaned, and Gerard was amazed as he entered the dining room. It was not as one would expect to find on a cattle station cum cheese factory. Dominating the room was a large oak table with high backed tapestry chairs.

Fine antiques were displayed to their best advantage in a tall glass cabinet, and as Jane dished up dinner,

Gerard browsed the many family portraits that hung on the walls in gilded frames, mainly of men sitting proudly on chestnut hunters and haughty women standing on the steps of English manors. One particular caught his interest, and he leaned in closer. It was definitely a younger Jane sitting amongst a group of well-to-do toffs with a red cocker spaniel by her feet.

"Good looking filly back in those days," said Max, coming to stand next to him. "That chap there," he pointed to a man with a heavy whiskered face, "is Lord Woodruff. Jane's father. Wearisome old bore. Didn't like it one bit when I swept her ladyship off her feet and she married a commoner."

"That's enough, Max," scolded Jane. "Father did come around in the end."

"Only after we had been married for twenty or so years."

"Let's not talk about that now," she said, as she pulled out a chair for Gerard. "Come," she said beckoning him to sit down.

When Gerard was seated, she moved to the doorway.

"Scherie," she called. "Come, dear. Dinner is ready."

"Cor Aunt," peeled a young girls voice, "I'm not eatin' in there. I'll have me dinner with the blokes."

"Suit yourself, dear, but we have a guest you know, and it is polite."

"Ah leave the girl be," cut in Max, "and sit your bum down."

Gerard relished every mouthful of the tender slabs of beef with fresh vegetables piled on his plate. Jane had made a trifle with custard laced with brandy, of which he and Max had more than one serving. Gerard doubted he could eat another mouthful. Jane began clearing the table, and Scherie popped in to give a hand.

"My niece," said Max, as way of introduction to the young girl dressed in a pair of frayed dungarees. Her small, pointed face was a mask of freckles, and no amount of cutting would ever tame the coiled curls of red hair that sprung around her face.

After Scherie left the room, Max gave a chuckle. "She be the death of Jane for sure, because she'd love nothing better than to see Scherie trussed up in frilly dresses and bows, but she's a real little tomboy, that one."

Gerard gathered that Scherie was about twelve years old and asked, "Does she go away to school?"

"No. Jane teaches her here, and what a battle she has on her hands!" Max gave a hearty laugh. "Jane is determined that Scherie will speak the King's good English, but that's a losing battle. Scherie spends most of her time out in the paddocks with the stockmen, so you can imagine the words she comes home with that aren't in Jane's dictionary."

Max glanced over at the liquor cabinet behind. His face broke into a wide grin. "She's left it unlocked!" he said rising to his feet. "Keep watch."

Max removed a crystal decanter and held it up to the light. "It's Jane's best brandy," he whispered, then grumbled, "but the blasted woman has marked the bottle."

He showed the tiny red dot to Gerard. "Quick! Pass us over those tea cups."

Max topped the cups up then placed the decanter back. He gave a nod. "Follow me. We'll drink this outside. Jane will think we're just havin' a cuppa… and if we drink up quick, we may just get a second snifter in before she comes back and locks the cupboard up."

"Surely she's not that harsh," remarked Gerard, as they settled themselves on the veranda step.

"She never used to be," Max leaned forward, looked around and then settled back. "She took Scherie back to England to see a burns doctor. Well, Dobson happens to drop by, and we polished off all the grog we had then. We got stuck into her brandy that she keeps for those toffs, then later we filled the decanter with cold tea."

Max gave a deep throated chuckle.

"Damned if I didn't forget, and blow me down, when she comes back, she's got that lot in tow with her… Her blasted Uncle kicked up a helluva row, and Jane was as nasty as a she dingo when she found out there was not a sniff of booze left on the station to offer them. Just cold tea." Max gave Gerard a dig in the ribs. "Damn woman had me sharing the bunk house with Dobson for a week over that little lot."

They sat talking for a long time, mainly about city life, until Max succumbed to weariness, and with an early start the next morning, he wandered off to bed Gerard stayed behind, gazing up at a star filled sky and listening to the raucous laughter drifting over from the stockmen's quarters. Knowing Dobson was amongst them, and with his love of ale, Gerard was certain that there would be some sore heads in the saddle the next day.

Chapter 9

Someone tapping on his door roused Gerard from a peaceful sleep. He wondered who it might be. Dobson perhaps? He then immediately discarded that idea, because Dobson was not one to stand on ceremony. Maybe Max, but he would be more the type to pound the door, so that left Jane.

"I'll just be a moment," he called climbing out through a swathe of mosquito netting. Putting his trousers on, then battling his way into a half-buttoned shirt, Gerard opened the door to Scherie standing there holding a cup of tea.

"Aunty's up the back shed milking goats," she greeted brightly.

"Oh," said Gerard, blinking his surprise. Was he expected to pay his way by going to help milk the goats or chase them around the paddock? He hoped not. Just the thought of it sent his muscles into a spasm.

Scherie placed a stained tin mug, one that looked as though it had come from the mustering camp, onto the table. "Aunt told me when I see you up, I have to bring you a cuppa." She gave him a cheeky grin. "I see you're up, so there's your cuppa."

"That's kind of you, Scherie," Gerard said, but when he tasted the tea, it was cold and well stewed, so he placed it back down.

"Aunt said if you are hungry, I have to cook you some breakfast."

"Now that was a good idea," thought Gerard. Scherie could well redeem herself for waking him up with cold tea by cooking him some fried eggs, lightly cooked, with perhaps a chop or bacon, toast cooked on the fork in the hot coals.

"Sure hot day." Scherie fanned her face and pushed her hair back from her freckled forehead. "Real hot place that kitchen. Yeah. Real bloody hot. Her shoulders sagged. "I've been cookin' since sun up."

She asked with a woebegone look. "You still want me to cook breakfast?"

Gerard resigned himself with the cold cup of tea, then excused himself to go to the bathroom. On his return, she was still there, sitting cross-legged on the floor staring at the distant mountain ranges.

"So Scherie," he asked as he sat down, "Were you born on this station?"

"Nope. I was born on High Rocks," she said. She raised an arm pointed north, and as she did, the sleeve of her blouse rolled down, and Gerard looked aghast at the purple and puckered burn scars running down her underarm.

She dropped her arm but spoke openly of her disfigurement. "I got burnt when I was a little girl, but I don't remember much." She pulled up one leg of her dungarees. "See, here too, this happened when my father burnt the house down, or so Dobson reckons. He took me out of the fire, but my mum died in the fire."

Gerard gently replied: "That's very sad, Scherie."

But it seemed the tragedy played a very small role in her life. She spun around on her buttocks and gave Gerard a cheeky smile. "I know a secret." she said.

"A secret?" Gerard's eyes widened. "Can I know? I'm very good at keeping secrets. That's my job… Keeping secrets."

Scherie put a finger on her lips. "It's a big secret."

She looked around making sure no one was close by. Her eyes fell serious. "If I tell, you are not allowed to tell anyone."

"I promise," replied Gerard, going along with the game.

"My daddy thinks I'm dead and buried too." She sprung to her feet. "Well, I gotta go now and help Aunty with the milking."

She bounced down the steps, leaving Gerard somewhat mystified. "What a strange little girl," he thought.

"I'm here, Aunty," called Scherie, as she wandered into the milking shed.

Jane sat on a short stool milking one of the goats. She turned around and gave an indulgent smile. "Have you had your breakfast dear? I left a plate for you on the stove."

"Yes, Aunty, and I ate it all. Oh, and that fellow staying here, he said he wasn't hungry, so I ate his too. But I made him a cup of tea."

"You're such a good girl," beamed Jane, then returned to her milking, while Scherie picked up a full pail of milk and emptied it into a wooden vat.

Not having children of her own, Jane was thankful for Scherie, but she always had a dreaded feeling that one day, her father would come to know that the child he thought had died in the fire actually lived not far from him. He was such a conceited ass and thankfully had little or no interest in anyone but himself. Jane pushed those thoughts aside; they only made her anxious.

When they had finished their work in the shed, Scherie released the goats to the paddock, and Jane returned to the homestead to prepare lunch. When Gerard was called, Jane gave some doubting looks to Scherie as Gerard ate with the gusto of a man that had not eaten breakfast.

As they cleared the table, Jane asked, "Gerard, would you like to saddle up one of the horses and go with Scherie for a ride around?"

Gerard declined, saying, "The only time I ever sat on a horse, I fell off it, and that happened to be my rocking horse. That experience soured me for life. Horses just don't seem to like me."

"That's 'cause you're ruddy scared of them," remarked Scherie candidly. "They smell it, you know, or so Billy reckons. And he'd know. He's the best horseman around."

"Scherie! How many times have I told you not to say…"

"Ruddy and bloody? Aunty, I try, but damned be the devil, you reckon I can stop?" replied Scherie, then skipped out of the kitchen.

As she carried the kettle to the sink, Jane gave an exasperated sigh. "What am I going to do with that child? Some days, I just don't know, and Max doesn't help, encouraging her to emulate the stockmen," she said. Jane poured water into a washing up bowl and Gerard picked up a tea towel.

"Don't worry, Jane. As my mother would say, it's probably just a phase she's going through."

"Gosh, I hope so," replied Jane, swirling a bar of soap around in the water. "Max and I were hoping to send her away to school next year." She gave a rueful grin. "But we say that every year, and every year, we find excuses to keep her near. Yet, she really needs other girls to play with."

Gerard wiped a plate and put it carefully on the table. "Not that I know a great deal about children, Jane, but Scherie seems a very bright little girl to me."

Jane smiled. She handed him a soapy plate. "I hope you don't mind me asking, but are you married?"

"Not yet. I think my job scares women away, or at least I hope it's my job, but I'm never in one place long enough to form a lasting relationship."

"What a charming man," Jane thought, making a mental note to tell all her suitable female friends.

She said, "Later this afternoon, I have to take some supplies out to the camp. Would you care to come along?"

"Love to, Jane." Gerard hung the tea towel up. Spotting the scrap bucket, he asked, "This for the chooks?"

"Yes, but be careful of the rooster. He gets a bit cranky."

Gerard left swinging the bucket. "It is a good life out on the station," he thought, but then he wasn't the one out mustering or doing any of the hard yakka.

Skirting around the back of the homestead, he made a beeline for the chook pen, where the hens, recognising the bucket, came babbling like little old women to the gate. Gerard unlatched the gate, opened it carefully, then shut it smartly when the rooster in residence came at him in attack, flying and squawking angrily over the heads of the hens. Never wishing to be a threat to any man's domain, Gerard tossed the lot, scraps and bucket over the fence then backed away.

"Better to do battle with Dobson than that rooster," thought Gerard, as he headed over to the quarters in search of him.

With the men away mustering, the quarters lay in shrouded silence. Stepping up onto the porch, Gerard opened a door and looked in to a long row of metal bunk beds with mattresses rolled and tied at the foot of each. There was no sign of Dobson or his swag. He tried another door, but it housed the tack, with bridles hanging on hooks and a ripped saddle resting up against the wall. He closed the door then wandered around to the back. He called out, but nobody answered.

"Perhaps Jane would know where Dobson was," he thought.

But Dobson had not slept the night at the homestead. When the stockmen had called it a night, he had hoisted his swag onto his shoulders and headed to the bush to sleep under the stars. Come morning, he wandered over to his mate's camp to have a bit of a yarn. They had sat, grogging on beneath a bush shelter made of branches and corrugated tin, and watched the kids run around in wild abandonment beating the tops of bushes with long sticks.

When the bottle of plonk was finished, Dobson decided to return to the homestead. He was hoping for a lift back, but the only ride coming along was heading in the other direction. He groused about that but continued walking, arriving back at the homestead in time to see Jane, Gerard and Scherie ready to leave in the cart.

"Oi," he shouted at half a run, "Where you lot going?"

"We're taking supplies out to the mustering camp," replied Gerard, and seeing Dobson's swag asked, "Where have you been?"

"Out walking. That's me job."

"Would you like to come along?" asked Jane.

"No, missus. I need to get a bit of shut eye before that mob come rollin' back in."

"There's food in the safe," she said, giving the reins a little slap on the ponies back. "Help yourself. We will be back about four."

"Changed me mind, Aunty," yelled Scherie from the back. "I'm gonna hang about a bit with Dobson."

Before Jane could protest, Scherie had jumped from the sulky and was running towards Dobson, who gave a shout with his hand in the air. "She'll be right, missus."

"What a strange man," thought Gerard, seeing Dobson take Scherie's hand. By the way Scherie's curly head kept bobbing up and down, he could imagine she was talking a mile a minute to the old swagman.

"Those two have a special relationship," said Jane, as she put the pony to a trot. She gave Gerard a long sideways glance. "She learns most of her bush skills from Dobson, and that old man would give his life for that child."

Gerard, settling into the rhythm of the ride, thought there was certainly a lot to this swagman that he did not know. Along the way, Jane pointed out many points of interest, which opened his eyes to the beauty of this vast land and its changing kaleidoscope of bush colours.

An hour on, they reached the mustering camp. Jane pulled the horse around in a wide circle and stopped near a tent. Nearby, cowpats were piled high, and Gerard felt pleased that he knew what they were used for.

The flap of the tent opened, and a man – obviously the cook, wearing a food-stained apron – called out as he came at a run.

"I'm sorry to have brought you out, missus, but it's blasted ants in the sugar again… Ah, beggin' me pardon," he said.

Jane swung down from the cart. "No need to apologise, Sam. I have the same problem back at the homestead, and anyway, I needed an outing."

She stood by as Sam and a helper unloaded the supplies. When they were ready to leave, Gerard was pleased to hear Jane say to Sam, on the pretext of her bread rising back at the homestead, that they did not have time for a cup of tea and a plate of kangaroo stew.

Chapter 10

Dinner that night in the homestead was less formal and somewhat sombre, with Max and Dobson eating in brooding silence. When dinner was finished, Jane and Scherie carried away the dishes and their conversation into the kitchen to discuss pickling and paring at length over the washing up.

When Max thought Jane was out of earshot he spoke up. "Dobson, did you speak to your mate about that little problem?"

"Yeah. I went to the camp last night. Had a bit of a yarn with him."

"And?" Max ducked his head sideways to look out the door. "What did he say?"

"Ya gotta wait till the bunyip man shows up in ya dreams. He'll tell ya what ya have to do, but I reckon a bullet—"

Gerard hearing the mention of a bullet and not wanting to share a cell with Dobson for some interminable period, immediately cut in. "What bullet! I hope you're not the cause of another problem, Dobson."

Max was quick to placate. "No. No. Nothing to do with Dobson… About my land and a… personal problem I am having. Nothing to worry about… really."

Gerard looked doubtful, and Dobson threw up his arms. "Nothing really, the man says. Huh! Fore ya know it, Max, ya missus will have nicked off, and you'll be campin' out in the bush with me for the rest of ya life!"

"Keep your voice down, Dobson!" hissed Max. He peered out the door towards the kitchen. "I don't want Jane to hear."

'Huh!" Dobson exclaimed as he stabbed the butter with a fork. "That woman would hear ya if we were yackin' down in the thirty-mile paddock! Only time a woman never hears ya is when ya tryin' to tell 'em something, then they are as bleedin' deaf as an old dog…"

"What's the problem, Max? Anything I can do to help?" asked Gerard.

"It's difficult, Gerard." Max ran a weary hand over his head. "Very difficult."

"Why not tell me how difficult?" replied Gerard.

Dobson pushed back his chair. "Let's all get out here, then you can tell him all about the mess we got ourselves in."

The very thought of a long incarceration with Dobson, and Gerard's eyes bulged.

"My office perhaps?" suggested Max.

Each with a glass in their hand, they tried to sneak past the kitchen, but Jane heard them and poked her head out the door. She looked suspiciously at the glasses.

"Just goin' to the office for some boy talk, my love." said Max.

"Well, don't stay up long, dear," she said, then smiled at Gerard. "I can't trust these two, but can you make sure all the lamps are turned off when you go to bed? Otherwise, I won't get a winks sleep."

"Women never bleedin' sleeps," growled Dobson, as they trouped into Max's office, a domain, thought Gerard looking around, that was obviously not considered Jane's.

He doubted she would have tolerated the untidiness of it all, with *Bushman's Gazettes* and newspapers piled high in the corner.

Max swept aside invoices, journals and unopened mail with his elbow to make room for a bottle of scotch on the table.

"Here you are, Gerard," he said, handing over a drink. "Oh, by the way, thanks for giving Jane a hand today."

"Ah flippin' heck, Max!" exclaimed Dobson, as he seized the neck of the scotch bottle. "You're as mean as ya missus with the grog! He topped his glass up.

"I don't wanna be here all night. Tell Billy Muggins 'ere about your problem." Max slouched over his chair.

"Ah shit! Then I'll tell him."

Max just gave a nod, and Dobson left his chair and came to perch on the edge of the table and closer to the scotch bottle. He looked at Gerard. "I'll try and make it as simple as ya can understand."

"From the beginning then, Dobson." replied Gerard.

"Well, it's like this. Max 'ere had a brother named Albert. Between 'em, they ran this station and had one of them fancy gentlemen's agreement, when later on down the track, someone gets to shaft the other bastard up the arse when they ain't lookin'. Now Albert got a son named Albert, but we call him Bertie, so when Albert died, Bertie got the lot. High Rocks and Kangaroo Downs, but not the gold mine, 'cause that's under lease."

Gerard took some moments to digest that information. He addressed Max, who sat gloomily running a finger around the rim of his glass. "I assumed you owned Kangaroo Downs, Max."

"Yes and no," replied Max taking up where Dobson had left off. "As you know, my father bought this land, and there was never an issue about who owned what, but when my father died, everything he owned reverted to his eldest son, which was my brother Albert."

"So," said Dobson, "Everything was fine for a couple of years until this lot decided takin' a wife each would be a good idea. That bein' Lady Jane and Bessie, but Bessie was a bit toey 'bout sharin' the same kitchen with her Ladyship, so to keep Bessie happy and give her a bigger kitchen, Albert built High Rocks."

Gerard massaged his temples. Max slammed his glass down.

"To cut a long story short Gerard," said Max, "both the stations are still under one land title, and now my nephew has it in mind that he wants to sell up, and if that's the case, there is nothing I can do about it."

Dobson spat. "He's just a little maggot, that one. I got no time for 'im! That Bessie spoilt him from the day he drew breath, but if I'd had my way, I would've stuffed a pillow over its ugly mug. Grizzlin' little shit, it was."

"He was always a difficult child," said Max. "I've tried talking to him, but he practically ran me off his land with a shotgun. Poor Emma. She was so distraught, but there was little she could do, because she is in a wheelchair."

"Who's Emma?" asked Gerard.

"She's my niece. A darling girl. Many times we have offered for her to come and live here, but she won't leave High Rocks."

"Anyways," cut in Dobson. "We got some interestin' info from me lady friend Maggie… She's me regular bit of fluff."

Max gave a warning look. "Let's not get into your love life, shall we?"

Dobson burped. "Yeah, right mate… Gets a bit messy down that track, huh… Anyway, Maggie says Bertie is headin' off to Perth. Probably wants to start the ball rollin' to sell off the place."

Gerard sat thinking for a few moments. "And you say there is a goldmine?"

"Yes, and it's a very lucrative one," replied Max. "But it hasn't been worked for some years. Bertie has been trying to lay his hand on that mine for some years now."

"And who has the rights to this goldmine?" asked Gerard. Giving Dobson a sceptical look, he raised his hand. "No, don't tell me... Let me guess, The Poet?"

Dobson gave a look of surprise. "Then yer not as bleedin' dumb as ya look, Billy Muggins."

"I was sorry to hear about him passing away," said Max. "I didn't really know him, but the odd times that I did meet him, he seemed a nice old chap."

"And now, with The Poet dead, the greedy little bastard wants to get his hands on that mine to boot."

"I doubt if we can stop that," remarked Max.

"Ya reckon, huh!" Dobson scrunched up his right eye. "The Weasel and I fixed him good on that score. He gotta prove The Poet is dead, and he can't do that 'cause he ain't got a body."

"And that's why you torched the shack," exclaimed Gerard. "'cause we bleedin' did. Whadda ya think we gonna do? Bury the poor bastard?"

Max looked stern. "Well, he probably would have appreciated a Christian burial. He could have been buried with his friend, what's his name… Tobias?"

Dobson gave a defiant look. "No room in that box for nobody. Not even Tobias!"

"What do you mean?" asked Gerard

"Simple, ain't it? The Poet always expected some bastard murdered Tobias, so instead of buryin' Tobias, he buried all their gold. That's where the Weasel and me went the other night. The Poet used to have to hang around waitin' for us to come to town so we could make his withdrawals from the cemetery bank."

Gerard and Max spoke in unison. "So where is Tobias?"

"Ah! The Poet tossed him down an old mineshaft… then buried all the gold in the coffin. Smart bastard The Poet."

Gerard was in need of a drink, but when he reached for the bottle, it was empty. He gave Max a concerned look. "What are your plans now?"

"Dunno yet."

So Gerard asked, "What about children? Does Bertie have any?"

That had Dobson erupting to his feet. "Ya diggin' ya shovel in deep there, mate. We ain't havin' her dragged into this mess… Poor kid she suffered enough."

Max held up his hand. "Dobson, be quiet. For just one minute, will you! This is where it gets complicated, Gerard. Some years back, Bertie went to Perth and arrived back with a… umm… what we expected was a lady of the night who was very pregnant. Rumour has it that they got married just before Scherie was born, but damned if we can find a marriage certificate or Scherie's birth certificate. Emma has been searching for them for years."

"Are these certificates so important?" asked Gerard.

"Definitely! Under my father's will, Bertie cannot sell the stations if there are children under the age of twenty-one, and Scherie is well under that. She's only eight years old."

"Hold on." Gerard shook his head to clear his thoughts. "Scherie's father is Bertie? The same man responsible for the burns Scherie received in the fire?"

Dobson sat morose. It was hard to hear him speak. "I thought she was dead," he mumbled. "She not even cryin' when I pulled her outta the fire. I just kept runnin' with her. No matter, I tell meself, dead or alive, you keep runnin', Dobson. Don't ya stop for no bastard, just keep runnin'. Get this little tucker to Jane."

Max gave a sorrowful shake of his head. "Bertie does not even know she's alive." He shifted uncomfortably in his chair. "She was only three years old at the time when Dobson brought her here. When we felt Scherie was strong enough, Jane fled with her to Perth for nearly a year. Later, when she came back with Scherie, everyone assumed we had adopted her."

"So, who knows the truth about Scherie?" asked Gerard, who was a little concerned remembering Scherie spoke openly to him, a stranger, about her past.

"Dobson, of course. Jane and Emma. We have never lied to Scherie about her parentage, but she knows she must always be cautious."

"Have you tried to gain copies of these certificates?" asked Gerard, logically.

Dobson scrunched up his right eye. "Yeah, but there's no record of 'em. I still reckon that Reverend Stoner married 'em both, but maybe Bertie didn't want to make it legal."

"Without those certificates," growled Max, "my hands are tied. I can't prove Scherie is his daughter and therefore cannot stop the sale, should Bertie want to proceed along that line."

The three men lapsed into thought. Gerard's thoughts centred around the power of the pen and bringing Bertie to ruin, while Max was concerned for Scherie and preserving her inheritance, and Dobson worried about the empty bottle in his hand.

Gerard had begun to hatch a plan. He spoke hesitantly. "High Rocks looking for new staff at all?"

"Don't really know," replied Max. "Why?"

"Well, an unknown face could always drop into High Rocks looking for work and do a bit of snooping around."

Dobson roared with laughter. "You? Ya don't know nothin' 'bout station work. Ya wouldn't know a fly blown arse if it was starin' ya in the face."

But Max wasn't ready to laugh that idea off so quickly. Gerard seemed to be an intelligent fellow. It wouldn't take much to teach him the basics of running a station, perhaps even gain Bertie's confidence.

Gerard's eyes slid to Dobson. "I'm willing to give it a try, but I'll need a backup."

"Me!" squealed Dobson. "No bleedin' way. I never want to set eyes on that man again."

"But you don't have to. He'll be in Perth."

Dobson clapped a hand to his head. "What fool neck scheme ya gettin' me into now, Billy Muggins?"

"What are you worried about, Dobson?" asked Max rising from his chair "I have to go and face the music now and tell Jane what's been going on."

Chapter 11

The following morning, a pair of riding boots, moleskin pants, thick sox and a hat had been left outside Gerard's door. Trying them on, he found the riding boots a bit tight, the moleskin pants stiff, but the hat was a perfect fit.

He clomped but, really wanting to swagger, made his way to the kitchen and thought he looked every bit the cattleman as he sat down at the table. Jane smiled as she dished him up breakfast, and Max gave a nod of approval. "Have you met Billy?" he asked, nodding to a well-muscled man also sitting at the table.

Billy rose, gave a quick "How ya goin' mate," picked up his hat then spoke to Max. "I'll get Queenie from the paddock. Reckon she's been spelled long enough out there."

"Yes, definitely." Max gave a thumbs up "A perfect choice for Gerard to learn on."

Gerard lowered his forkful of food. "To learn what on?" he asked

"Horse riding, of course!" boomed Max. "Otherwise, what sort of bushman would you be if you can't even sit a horse?"

"A live one," replied Gerard dryly.

Carrying a bowl of peas to shell, Jane came and sat down. She had her piece to say. "I don't like the idea of Gerard going anywhere near High Rocks," she said, giving Max's hand a slap as he dipped his fingers into the bowl of peas.

"Bertie is a ruthless man, and if he finds out we have sent Gerard there, goodness knows what he will do."

Dobson heaped sugar into his mug of tea. "Don't ya worry, Missus, about Billy Muggins 'ere. That's his job stickin' his snout into other people's business."

Gerard pushed his empty plate away. "Look at it this way. I would probably get myself into a lot more strife just sitting in the pub with Dobson all day than I would at High Rocks."

Jane fussed. "Hard to say which is the better of two evils, Bertie or Dobson."

"Forgot to mention," said Dobson, which Gerard found Dobson did a lot of: forgetting to mention.

"Took a ride out last night to visit me bit of—"

Max jumped in, "Maggie!"

"Yeah, Maggie. I told her to keep her eyes open for any mail comin' in or out."

This alarmed Jane, and she snapped angrily. "I forbid it. Really, this has gone too far! First Gerard, and now

Maggie, and should Bertie ever find out she is tampering with his mail, she will be done for!"

"Maggie and Emma?" Dobson gave a wicked grin. "Them two been doin' it for bleedin' years, and they ain't got caught yet."

He also dipped his hand into the bowl of peas, and she slapped Dobson's and Max's hand in turn. "Both of you, leave my peas alone! Wretched men."

"Yes, Dobson," said Max rising from his chair.

"Leave the peas alone." He snatched his hat off the peg and nodded to Gerard. "Billy should be in now with Queenie. We don't want the day to get away from us."

"And that's another thing," cried Jane, as the men filed out of the kitchen. "Gerard can't even ride a horse, and you're putting him on that dreadful mount."

Max placed a hand on Gerard's shoulder. "Don't listen to her, Gerard. Old Queenie's a good horse and very placid… most of the time."

Gerard had his doubts about this when Queenie was led around snorting and prancing at the end of the rein. She was a bay mare, with a white blaze running down her forehead, and stood at least seventeen hands high, dwarfing the other horses nearby.

"Hey, boss," shouted Billy as he danced around, "she's been in the paddock too long. Bit on the frisky side. Ya wanna take her out for a bit of a gallop first?"

Max eyed the mare dubiously. "Not me, Billy. What about you, Dobson?"

"Ya friggin' jokin!" Dobson backed away.

"Reckon it's gotta be me," said Billy, swinging up into the saddle. He took up the reins, and a gentle touch of the heel was all it took for Queenie to take off at a standing gallop.

"And you two have to be crazy," cried Gerard, "if you think I am going to get on that horse!"

And crazy they were when Billy galloped back and they hoisted Gerard into the saddle.

"Now, mate," crooned Billy to the fractious Gerard, "ya just stay up there, and we gonna have a bit of a walk around first."

Gerard closed his eyes, clutched a hold of some mane hair, slouched in the saddle and hung on tight. A number of turns around, and Gerard began to straighten up.

"Yep. A real pro," called Dobson laughing from the side lines. "Next, we'll have ya ridin' in one of them derbies and chasin' foxes across the paddocks."

"I think you mean fox hunting," remarked Max. "And they only do that in European countries."

"Well then, we'll 'ave him chasin' dingoes."

"I don't really feel safe up here," said Gerard, as he was led past.

"No flamin' worries, mate, you're doin' pretty good," remarked Billy, as he indicated another turn with his hand. "Now move yer' hips a bit, bloke. Just like ridin' yer' missus."

"Perhaps I would be better suited to a shorter horse," said Gerard. "A pony, perhaps, if there is one to spare."

Billy halted and gave the mare's neck a rub. "Queenie's the only horse we got to spare. Now let's do somethin' with them feet of yours."

"Ya gotta bend em," hooted Dobson, as Billy tried to bend Gerard's knees, but they remained rigid. Max moved forward and gave Gerard an undercut behind the knees.

"Now keep the tip of your boot in the stirrup," ordered Max. "No! Don't push your feet right through."

"Yer do that mate," remarked Billy, adjusting the position of Gerard's toes, "if ya horse bolts, you have to make sure ya can kick free from the stirrups. If ya come a cropper and ya feet are stuck, then you'll be ridin' with ya bloody head bouncin' on the ground and ya arse in the air, and that's how we'll bury ya, mate!"

Gerard considered the point well taken, and though he remained nervous, he did however at the end of his first lesson manage a trot without falling off.

When Gerard clumsily dismounted, the men applauded.

"Okay now, bloke," said Billy, "I'm gonna show ya how to unsaddle her, rub her down, then give her a feed. A week doin' that, and she'll be bloomin' right."

Being the night of the week when the boss shouted two free ales, the station men gathered around the kitchen and talked, mainly about Gerard's first riding lesson, and there was plenty of advice forthcoming from them on how it should be done. When the ales were finished, the men began drifting back to their quarters, but before Max took his leave, he told Gerard, "I'll be away mustering for a week or so. I'm leaving Billy behind. Just follow him around and learn as much as you can."

Billy proved to be a patient teacher, and Gerard spent most of his time with Queenie. He began to lose his nervousness of her and was happy when she would whinny to him when she saw him walking across to the stable yard.

The week passed quickly, with Billy announcing at the end of it, "I reckon ya can take Queenie out for a run on ya own." He pointed to a far-off windmill. "Mind, only to there and back. I'll just stand here and watch. If ya get yourself into trouble, I'll be there in a tick," he said, giving his horse – a shaggy looking brumby – a pat.

Gerard felt confident. He urged Queenie into a canter, and with the wind blowing through his hair, he felt a rush of exhilaration and forgot about his other world of printer's ink, meeting deadlines, cigar smoke, noisy trolley trams, buggies and pub fumes. Reaching the windmill, he did a neat turn around, then cantered back to Billy, who was observing from the homestead.

"Yer done real good," enthused Billy upon his return, and they walked to the stables. "You and Queenie, youse' gonna make a good team."

"Well, thank you Billy, that's a nice compliment and makes me feel less like the greenhorn that I really am."

"So damn good in fact the boss wants to give ya Queenie to keep."

"I couldn't possibly take this horse!" exclaimed Gerard.

"Yes, ya can." Billy gave him a resounding slap on the back. "You'd be doin' us a favour. None of the blokes 'ave got time for her. Too high bred for us. Shit!

We don't even let her share the same feed bag with our horses, in case they start gettin' uppity ideas and go on strike."

Gerard unsaddled Queenie, and as he ran the curry comb over her, he said to Billy, who stood looking on, "She's a beautiful horse."

Dobson appeared in the doorway, "No, she ain't!"

"She's a bleedin' bitch, that one," shouted Scherie, her curly head poking out around Dobson.

"Oi Dobson," called Billy. "I was gonna come lookin' for ya. Gerard made it to the windmill without fallin' off, so that'll be a bob of yours in me pocket if ya please."

Scherie turned her face and cupped her hand. "And threepence for me !" she demanded.

Chapter 12

When Max arrived home from his week-long muster, dusty and smelling of cow dung, he tramped up onto the veranda, flopped down on the step and tugged his boots off. He brooked no argument from Jane when he told her gruffly, "I've run out of my supply of brandy, and I need a good snort from that bottle you keep hidden away for medicinal purposes."

Picking up the offensive boots, Jane marched them away, and Max called after her, "And don't be tight fisted with that pouring arm of your either, Jane." He turned around and grinned at Gerard, who sat behind, reading a copy of the *Bushman's Gazette*. "I've had some good reports about you from Billy."

Jane returned with the bottle of brandy and two glasses. "Not for me, Jane," said Gerard, who – knowing the brandy was in short supply – tapped his glass of minted tea. "This will do me just fine."

Dobson, possibly catching a whiff from the brandy bottle, appeared and bounced up the steps. He snatched the bottle out of Jane's hands, but she snatched it back.

"Oh no, you don't, Dobson! That's the only bottle left, and I'm saving it for emergencies!"

"Well, I'm a bleedin' emergency!" he retorted, then in jest glared at Max. "See what happens when you lose control of ya woman. 'Fore ya know it, they start servin' ya grog in a thimble then start rabbitin' on about ya bein' a drunkard."

But Jane relented. She poured him a drink, but he protested, looking most desolately at his half-filled glass. "Can't ya do better than that?" But seeing her look and knowing not to push his luck too far, he slid down on the step and sat next to Max.

"Before I get drunk on this sniff of brandy and forget, Billy told me to tell ya, he's gonna check on a few windmills and wants to know if Wyatt Earp 'ere is up to ridin' along?"

"But that's more than a twenty-mile ride," remarked Jane, as she tucked the bottle under her arm and out of Dobson's reach.

Max turned around and looked at Gerard. "What do you think, Gerard? It's a long day and a hard ride. Do you think you are up for it?"

Placing his hands behind his head, Gerard stretched out his long legs. "So, Dobson, what's the betting in the bunkhouse?"

Dobson lifted his head and scratched his chin. "Well, half reckons ya'll never make the distance, quarter of 'em reckon ya will, and the rest are still makin' up their bleedin' minds about it."

Gerard dropped his hands and crossed his ankles. "And what about Billy? How's he betting?"

"He's puttin' up the bank on this one, reckon either way, he can't lose on ya." Max laughed. "What about you, Dobson? Which way are you betting?"

"I reckon ya can't do it."

Immediately, Gerard rose to the challenge. "Then maybe I'll just surprise you, Dobson."

"And that's a bob in me pocket," thought Dobson smugly, "for gettin' the silly blighter to go along."

The next morning, the usual cloudless blue day dawned, and Gerard was ready when Billy came looking for him. As they rode out to the windmills, Billy again proved to be a patient teacher, explaining in detail the mechanics of how a windmill ran, how to grease the pumps and blow the lines clear so there was always a supply of trickling water going into the troughs.

"The next windmill," said Billy, as he packed his tools away, "is all yours."

The horses were tired, so Billy instructed they keep them at a walk. And just when Billy thought things were going his way, a small bush rat scuttled out of the bush. Billy's horse stood firm, but Queenie laid her ears back flat and reared up high.

"Bloody Strewth!" shouted Billy, making a lunge for her reins, but he missed.

Queenie landed down heavily on her front hooves, tossed her head, then bolted out across the paddock.

Gerard, in his panic, had lost hold of one rein, and it dangled dangerously between Queenie's front legs.

He swayed in the saddle and heard Billy shout, "Kick yer feet outta the stirrups!"

Just seconds later, he tumbled out of the saddle.

It was not Billy's practice to use the spurs on any horse, but he did this time and dug in hard, because he knew should Queenie take a fall, it would have to be a bullet to her head for sure.

Queenie proved no match for the seasoned little brumby that galloped up behind, then drew abreast and close enough for Billy to leap from one saddle to the other. Immediately, the brumby dropped back and galloped on behind.

Moving high up on the mare's neck, Billy leaned out sideways and seized both trailing reins up. He snatched them up, then looped them around the mare's neck. Leaning out, he grabbed hold of Queenie's bit and began wheeling her around until he finally gained control of the runaway horse. He cantered back to Gerard, who lay motionless on the ground.

Tying Queenie to a nearby tree, he ran to Gerard and came sliding in beside him. "How bad you hurt, mate?" he asked.

Gerard groaned. Billy ran his hands expertly over Gerard, feeling for any broken bones. He couldn't detect any, but that wasn't to say that Gerard had not encountered some other injury to his body or head. He then knelt behind Gerard's head and supporting his neck said, "Slowly, now. Just try to come up easy, bloke."

Gerard struggled to a sitting position, and Billy was relieved. "Now move yer feet slowly, bloke," he said and watched closely as Gerard rotated his right foot then his left foot, but he gave a wince at that.

"That's okay, bloke. Now I want you to roll your shoulders."

But when Gerard did, he screamed in pain and grabbed his left shoulder. He howled in agony when Billy, with a few twists and turns, manipulated his shoulder back into place. When Gerard finished howling and began cursing and spitting Billy knew he'd be okay.

"Now, bloke," Billy gave him a worried look, "you reckon you're okay to get back in the saddle?"

And as Gerard struggled to his feet and hobbled towards his horse, Billy had to admire the grit of this city slicker.

Back at the homestead, Jane kicked up one helluva to do as she bandaged Gerard's shoulder, and when he was resting comfortably propped up in bed with pillows behind, she intoned a royal order. "Except to eat and rest, you are not to do anything strenuous for at least three days. Unless, of course, I tell you to do so."

"I feel like an invalid," he told Max when he came visiting, but Max just grinned.

"You've made Jane's day! She loves nothing better than to fuss over the sick and injured. It gives her the powers of being to be a right bossy boots."

When Dobson heard the word that the journo bloke had come a cropper, he was his usual sympathetic self. "Ya bloody drongo! What ya go and do a fool arse thing like that for?"

As for Scherie, standing next to him, she screwed up her nose and piped, "Yeah! Now me and Dobson are down ten bob 'cause yer' a bleedin' Nancy and come a cropper off ya horse."

On the third day, Jane allowed him out of bed.

"Good to see you up and about," remarked Max, when Jane helped him into the kitchen, followed by Dobson, who shouted, "Mail delivery!" Then he tossed a pile of letters on the kitchen table.

Max picked up the letters and frowned as he rifled through them. He dropped them back on the table. "Dobson, this is not my mail! This is Bertie's mail. I can't possibly open the man's mail."

"Knew you'd say that, so I already done it for yer," replied Dobson, as he came to stand by Max's shoulder. Leaning over, he fanned the letters out, then flicked one across to Gerard. "This'll interest you! I just got yer a job on High Rocks, as the new station manager."

Max moved to sit next to Gerard, and both men poured over the letter that Bertie had written, confirming to a Mr Mark Reynolds that his application as station manager for High Rocks Station had been accepted and asking if he could make his way to High Rocks as soon as possible, because he had urgent business to attend to in Perth.

"Oh yeah, I nearly forgot." Dobson lifted his shirt and pulled out a long envelope that was tucked into the waistband of his pants. "Have a gander at this, but be quick. I gotta get it back to Maggie in case Bertie goes lookin' for it."

Max carefully smoothed out the letters, and Gerard sorted through the numerous recommendations from employers obviously pleased with this man Mark Reynolds as a valued employee.

"Pretty damn impressive," remarked Max when they had read all. "But damned if I know why Bertie would want a sheep man working for him. This man has had little or no experience working with cattle."

Gerard stabbed a finger halfway down the page of one particular letter. "I don't think it's his experience with cattle that Bertie is interested in. Look. Right here, it says amongst other things, that he managed a gold mine in Kalgoorlie."

Max slammed his fist on the table. "So that's Bertie's sneaky little game. He's after someone to run the goldmine."

Jane, with her mouth pursed, had remained silent, making tea and cutting up a date loaf, but she muttered as she handed tea and cake around: "I still don't like it. And now we're sending an invalid to High Rocks. Dobson, are you having a cuppa?"

Dobson gave a disdainful look at the mug. "Now if you'd offer a man a brandy, I'd be the first to put me hand up."

"Which I'm not." she snapped.

'He's just a bleedin' Nancy," grumbled Dobson, looking enviously into his empty mug.

Chapter 13

They sat up well into the night discussing the pros and cons of Gerard actually impersonating Mark Reynolds or just going to High Rocks on the pretext of looking for work. Finally, after much debate, they agreed the best option was that of pretending to be the new station manager applicant.

"Oh damn, I forgot to mention," said Dobson, who – having spent the night out collecting the mail – lay sprawled in his chair half asleep. "That letter was wrote some weeks ago. Bertie been expecting that blighter any day, or so he reckoned to Ruby who told Maggie who told me."

"Well, I'd say we have about two weeks up our sleeves to teach Gerard what has taken me thirty years!" Max said, frowning dourly at Dobson and wagging a finger. "And don't you go laying bets either. And while I'm on the subject of gambling, there's Scherie! Should Jane come to know she has been sitting in on a few rounds of poker down at the quarters, you'll get more than what for from her!"

'We were not teachin' the little tyke to play poker! We were teaching her arithmetic."

"I bet you were," replied Max, then turned slightly away to hide his grin. "But Jane is correct in what she says," he thought. "Scherie does get out of hand when Dobson is around; but then, and even he had noticed, the child's moody spells became less frequent."

Over the next five days, Gerard was pushed physically and mentally to his limit. He went to bed every night exhausted, and Jane remarked often that he was trimming down. His office flab had become toned muscle and having lost his city pallor, he had become bronzed from days working in the sun. His hair was now sun streaked, and he felt fit; so fit in fact that he was thinking about taking that cranky old rooster on.

Then it came time to leave.

Max rode with him to the boundary and aired his last minutes concerns, but Gerard waved then aside. "Don't worry about me, Max. If I hit a sticky patch, I'll take a leaf out of Dobson's book and bullshit my way through."

When Gerard rode into High Rocks Station, he was shocked to see the place in such disrepair. He hitched Queenie to a pole and walked up to the main house with a yard that was overgrown with weeds. The place had an unwelcoming feel about it, as did the two dogs that hurtled out from under the veranda and came at him with raised hackles and gnashing of teeth. Lucky for Gerard, they ran out of rope.

"Bloody mongrels!" he shouted, then lashed out with a booted foot, which only incited the dogs into another fit of frenzied barking. Bertie working in his office and hearing the dogs and Gerard came outside to investigate. Not recognising Gerard, he shouted, "Who are you, and what do you want?"

Gerard looked over. "This is him," he thought, given Bertie's family resemblance to Max.

"I'm Mark Reynolds, your new station manager, and if you don't shift those bloody dogs, I'll give them both a bullet!"

"Bugger off!" commanded Bertie. The dogs immediately turned and skulked back under the veranda to lay in wait for the next victim to come along.

Bertie came forward, "Sorry about that."

"And so you should be," replied Gerard. He pointed to the two black noses jutting out from under the veranda. "That's your dogs' names? Bugger and Off!"

Bertie gave a girlish laugh. "Everyone used to tell them to bugger off as pups, and now that's all they answer to." He stuck his hand out. "I'm Albert Nightingale," he said, "but you can call me Mister Nightingale."

Gerard returned the handshake.

"And I'm Mark Reynolds," he said, then grinned broadly. "But you can call me Lord Reynolds if you like, Bertie."

"Oh." Bertie was momentary lost for words. "Is that a joke?"

"Yeah!" replied Gerard gruffly. "Now, where's my quarters. I've ridden a long way."

"One moment," Bertie said, looking around. He spoke under his breath, "Where the dickens is that woman!" Then he yelled, "Ruby! Get out here."

From around the side of the house, a woman of rather large proportion and wearing a red and white spotted smock ambled towards them. Perched on her shoulder was a white crested cockatoo. "You callin' me, boss?" it squawked.

"I was out the back," said Ruby.

Bertie pointed to Gerard. "This is the new station manager Mark Reynolds. Show him to the manager's house." He turned to Gerard. "When you've settled in, come back, and we'll have a little chat."

"Meet Sailor," said Ruby, transferring the bird from her shoulder to her wrist. The cockatoo's head jiggled up and down, and he screeched, "Ship ahoy! Cast anchor."

As Ruby led the way to a clutch of buildings set some distance from the house, the bird kept up its seafaring monologue. Ruby stopped outside a small wooden house with a tin roof and no door. "This is the manager's quarters," said Ruby, and Sailor squawked 'Man overboard! Man overboard!"

Gerard found the bird to be highly entertaining. "Does the bird ever shut up?" he asked.

"Do you?" she snapped, as she drew aside a faded curtain hanging from the doorway.

Gerard followed her into a small airless room with battered furniture. He looked around, and knowing Dobson would not even camp here, he walked out.

"Where are you going?" shouted Ruby as she waddled after him. "You ain't seen the rest of the place."

"Man overboard," screeched the bird, fluttering up in the air a few feet, then down again to perch on Ruby's head.

Gerard abruptly stopped and turned around. "I assume the main house has a guest bedroom?"

'Yeah, we gotta a couple," she replied sulkily.

"Good! Then I suggest you hunt down a mop and broom and give my room up there a bit of a spruce up." He pointed over to a shed with a horse yard. "I assume that's where I can keep my horse?" he asked.

Gerard returned to the ramshackle manager's house, collected Queenie and led her over to the yard. Unsaddling her, he carried her tack into a nearby shed, where he found feed bins, buckets, brushes and a currycomb. Gerard busied himself by emptying the dirty water trough, then carried fresh water from a tank at the side of the shed. When he had fed her, he had a quick tub himself by the tank stand, then headed back to the main house.

There was no one around, so he went into the kitchen and looked around in disbelief at the dirty dishes piled on benches and half-filled pots of what looked like watery stew sitting on the stove that smelt sour from being soaked too long.

The table was a battlefield of food where flies swarmed, hovered or died drowning in the melted yellow butter that Ruby was too lazy to put away.

He opened his mouth and roared, "Ruby!"

Dragging a broom behind her, she came to the kitchen door. "Yeah, what ya want?" she snarled.

"Get this mess cleaned up," he ordered, and in answer to this, she threw the broom down.

"Ya want I do all the work, then I tell ya right now, Mister, I gonna be on the next cart outa' here!"

"That's the best suggestion I've heard all day," replied Gerard, and he left the kitchen to go in search of Bertie to have that promised chat with him.

Chapter 14

Gerard had never been in anyone's office that did not have at least a notebook on the table, but he had now, as he pulled up a chair in Bertie's office. Placing his hands casually behind his back, he said, "Well, I'm here for that little chat."

Bertie blinked in disbelief. He wasn't used to people just walking casually unannounced into his office, then making themselves comfortable, least of all the hired help.

Crossing his legs, Gerard rested his right knee at a comfortable angle. He inspected his fingernails for a few seconds, then spoke. "Before I say my piece, I'll listen to what you have to say first."

Bertie blustered. "Well, I'm a bit surprised…"

"Why?" replied Gerard. "You invited me for a chat."

"Oh yes. Well, first, you've come highly recommended from Bob Terrel down in Suhum. You worked for him, how long, until he died… Eight years?"

Gerard raised his hands above his head, linked his fingers, stretched then dropped his arms. "His name is Bob Turnvil, not Terrel, and I worked for him for four years. He hasn't died – well, not yet – but he retired a few months back, and as I told you in my letter, I am more of a sheep man myself." That, Gerard thought, was no lie considering the number of woollen suits he owned.

Bertie was not used to being treated with such impertinence. "You're pretty bloody sure of yourself, aren't you, Mister Reynolds?"

Gerard gave a slow smile. "Well, as you said, I have come highly recommended, and with my experience and expertise in a number of fields, it is not hard for me to find employment. I only took this job on because I needed a change of scenery from working down south, but I'm more interested in furthering my experience working the mine that you said you had."

Bertie frowned. He was unsure how to take this man, but like him or not, he needed him. "Well, Mark, first, let me welcome you to High Rocks. As I had mentioned in my letter to you, I am away quite a bit."

"So that explains the shambles this station is in, then?" said Gerald.

"It's my overseer, you see," replied Bertie. "He does a fair enough job on the land and keeps the men in line. I really need you for the managerial side of things."

Gerard nodded. He had to agree with him, since he considered himself better qualified at pen pushing than pushing bulls through a pen.

"I'm also happy to give you a free run of the place, say three months," said Bertie with a raised eyebrow.

"Sounds fair to me."

"That's good," replied Bertie, "because I'm off to Perth tomorrow, so you can start then." He rose, indicating the interview was over and looked mildly surprised when Gerard remained seated.

"Now that you have had your say," drawled Gerard lazily, "it's my turn to tell you how it's going to be. First, I'm moving up to the main house, and second, that Ruby. She has to go."

Gerard kept Bertie for nearly an hour, and when he decided the interview was over, he swaggered out of the office with an air of a man who knows what it's all about.

The following morning, as Bertie was packing up the buggy, he mentioned his sister Emma. Gerard feigned surprise. "I didn't know you had a sister living here. I haven't seen her around yet, but we'll probably run into each other sometime during the day."

"Oh, I doubt that, since she's in a wheelchair. She has this woman Maggie who sees to all her needs, and they have their own living quarters, over there by the trees, separate from the main house."

Gerard looked in the general direction of where Bertie was indicating and through the trees glimpsed a tall smoke stack and a patchwork quilt of red brick.

Bertie tossed the last bag into the buggy and climbed aboard. Gerard thought he was running an eye over the mountain of bags, as if he was planning to return.

"I've left you a list in my office of a few things I need you to do and my house address in Perth where I will be staying."

"You have a house in Perth?" Gerard looked towards the house. "Then why don't you take Ruby along with you to keep house?"

"Don't be ridiculous, man!" Bertie flicked his whip, and the horse and buggy took off, leaving Gerard standing in the dust.

When the buggy was out of sight, Gerard started to make his way back inside the house. He had a determined look on his face. "First things first," he said aloud, "and that is to sort that bloody Ruby out!"

But when he approached the kitchen, he had another welcoming committee waiting for him. This time, it was a group of angry men.

"You the new manager?" called out one man.

"Depends what the problem is," replied Gerard, coming to stand in front of them.

"Well, she's the bloody problem!" retorted the self-elected spokesperson, pointing to Ruby parked up under a tree sleeping off the grog. "Now, whaddya gonna do about it?" he said, as he jammed a cigarette in the corner of his mouth.

Gerard stared down at Ruby, who snored and drooled. The cockatoo lay next to her, on its back with its legs in the air. "Are they sick?" asked Gerard. "Perhaps we should send for a doctor?"

"She ain't sick! By the way, me name's Tubby."

Gerard nodded, then remarked, "Well, it's a bloody shame the boss has already shot through. He could've dropped her off along the track!"

A tall, weather-beaten man came out of the kitchen shouting. "I know where I'd like to drop her off!" He looked at Gerard. "I'm Lionel, the overseer," he said, "and if we don't do something about Ruby and the grub she serves up, then the lads 'ere are already talkin' about walkin' off the job."

"Well," remarked Gerard candidly. "Who can blame them for that?" He peered around Lionel and into the kitchen. "I see she has made an effort to clean up at least."

"She's made an effort all right." said Lionel glaring at Ruby's form. "She bloody well tossed all them dirty plates and pots, the whole bloody lot down the thunderbox out back!"

Gerard shook his head in disbelief. "Oh shit!"

"And that's exactly what they're swimming' in now mate, out there in the thunderbox," roared Lionel.

The men broke into an angry squabble. Gerard held his hands up. "Now, come on, boys," he pleaded, "give me a break. I've only just arrived."

"He's right," said Lionel backing him up. "Give the bloke a go at least."

Grudgingly, the men became silent but their anger hung heavy.

"We can all stand around here complaining and get nothing done, or we can pull together and get something done. What's it to be, then?" said Gerard addressing the men.

The men hung their heads and shuffled their feet.

Gerard asked looking around at the po-faced men. "Anyone of you had any cooking experience?"

"Oh damn and hell!" said one stepping forward. "I did a spell down south as a shearer's cook. I s'pose I can give a hand here until the next cook arrives. They call me Noddy," he said, giving Gerard's hand a shake.

"Come on, now," said Lionel, "let's make a start and get this bloody kitchen cleaned up."

Noddy, it seemed, had broken the ice, and the men must have liked the look of this new manager, because quickly between them, they began to organise a work detail.

Gerard donned an apron, Lionel and a ringer named Blue went to borrow what cooking pots and kitchen utensils that Maggie could spare, while Harry and Bert hauled a large metal tub from the laundry and filled it with water. The rest of the work detail scouted around for brushes, brooms and anything else that could be used in the kitchen, while Reg and Mick took off to the hen house carrying back eggs in their hats. The storeroom produced some spuds and onions, which along with the eggs was enough to cook the men a feed.

Over breakfast, Gerard yarned with Lionel. "First thing we have to do is bring food supplies in."

Lionel readily agreed. "But you're lookin' at two days if we gotta go to Ullaging. I reckon the best is we send a couple of blokes into Dawkins today, and they can pick us up enough to see us through for a couple of days and send another two with the cart into Nullagine."

"And meat?" asked Gerard.

Lionel rubbed his chin. "There's plenty of roo out in the paddocks. I'll find a steer later and do a kill, but the meats gotta hang for a couple of days and get salted."

Gerard drummed his fingers on the table. "What we need is a regular order coming in, say, every two weeks. How do we go about organising that?"

"The boss got an account at the General Store, also one in Dawkins. He pays every month, but he's a tight-arsed bastard that one. Hates spendin' money unless it's on himself."

When the men had left to go to work, Gerard – recalling Jane's well stocked storeroom – began taking stock and penning a long list.

When Noddy checked the store's list that Gerard had compiled, he gave a long whistle as he saw it ran to a number of columned pages. "The boss gonna have a right old fit over this lot."

"That's gotta be around two hundred quid's worth of stores . Bastard can afford it," grumbled Noddy, as he pocketed the list. "I'll send a couple of the boys in today."

Lionel picked up his hat. "Mate," he said, looking straight at Gerard, "I wanna have a word with you in private. Outside is a good place."

They stood outside, and Gerard asked, "What's the problem then, Lionel?"

"The problem, mate, is that horse of yours."

"Queenie?"

"Yeah, mate. I had to shift her this morning from the yard."

"Why is that?" asked Gerard. "Was she causing a problem?"

"Well, she would have," replied Lionel, "if the boss had gotta look at the brand on her arse and seen she come from Kangaroo Downs!"

He looked Gerard fair square in the eye.

"Listen, mate, I don't reckon you are really this Mark Reynolds bloke. I'll be straight with ya, mate. I don't give a tuppeny shit about the boss, but I do about Miss Emma. I promised her dad that I'd look out for her, no matter what, and what I got in me gut is a feelin' something is on the boil around this place. I been feelin' it meself for some time. If me gut feelin' is right and this got somethin' to do with Max, then ya got me backing one hundred bloody percent."

Chapter 15

Dobson continued to trudge along the track. He stopped to wipe the last of the day's sweat from inside the brim of his battered old felt hat. Some miles on, he veered off into the bush fronting the Pilbarra area.

It was near dusk. The first purple shafts of the dying sun pierced the dry caked mud on the creek bed. Once across, he sat down on a small boulder to empty his boots of the gritty sand and small pebbles, then retrieved the bottle of Muscat from his swag and drank alone, listening to the sounds of night closing in.

Holding up the bottle of Muscat, he toasted his old mate The Poet and hoped Tobias had been putting in some good words upstairs for the silly old bugger. "Poor bloody Tobias," he said to himself, "he was a harmless old bugger, and what a way to meet his end."

Dobson thought back.

The night Tobias had died, they'd been drinking at the pub. Tobias had left early, as he and The Poet continued on drinking and arguing, as drunks do.

Later that evening, when their mate Curly had dropped in to borrow a pick, he found Tobias dead on the floor, lying in a pool of blood. The Poet needed to know, so Curly had borrowed Tobias' donkey, since Tobias wouldn't need her anymore, and trotted into town.

When Curly arrived at the pub he went straight into the bar, seeing Curly without a glass in his hand, Robert pounced. "An ale, Curly?" he asked

"No, mate," replied Curly, "I need a heart starter."

"Oh, problem with the old ticker, then?" remarked Robert, placing the brandy glass down.

"Not mine, mate. Tobias. He's the one with a problem with his ticker."

"How so?" Robert had asked.

'It ain't tickin' no more." Curly tossed back the brandy. "The Poet about? Need to tell him his mate is dead and if he wanna sell me that old donkey now that Tobias won't be needin' her no more."

Robert looked around the bar for The Poet but couldn't see him anywhere. "Well, I can't see him. He was over there before, drinking with Dobson… Hold on, there's Fred. Since he's the undertaker, better you have a word with him."

"Yeah." Curly nodded to his empty glass on the bar. "First, I gotta get meself a second wind. I've had a helluva shock, ya know!"

"Well, while you're getting your wind up," said Robert, untying his apron and slinging it over the bar, "I'll just nip out back and tell Kathleen to tend bar, then I'll pop over to the post office and send a telegram to the Nullagine coppers. They need to know."

The Poet took the news about Tobias very hard, with Kathleen calling for the doc and then putting him to bed. She couldn't stay with him and was pleased when the laudanum took effect, and she had to get back to the bar, busy now with everyone having something to drink to.

Robert didn't send that telegram, as he said he would, but he took the buggy and went over the ridge to Tobias' place.

The trip at night was a dangerous one, and the horse balked at shadows or stones clattering on down the mountainside that fell from the wagon wheels.

But Robert had only one thing on his mind: to find the mining lease. He'd be a millionaire, he knew. And The Poet, well, he'd deal with him later. Continually, he whipped the horses on.

The shack was in darkness when Robert pulled up front, which it would be, thought Robert, as he jumped from the cart, since Tobias had already found himself another guiding light.

The door was open, and inside all around was pitch black. Robert walked in, tripped over Tobias laying sprawled on the floor, and when he had recovered from his fall, lit a match. He saw a candle on the table, set that to light and then began hunting around. His search turned up nothing, and he feared he had wasted a trip. But maybe not? He looked down at Tobias. He could do with extra business, so why not bury this old bastard himself. The Poet could well afford his price.

Hoisting the dead miner over his shoulder, he carried him outside and dumped him unceremoniously in the back of the buggy, but Tobias, a tall man, didn't quite fit, and no amount of pushing and prodding would make him do so. He didn't want the old man bouncing out of the cart and over the ridge and thought, "Nothing else to do but tie him up front."

Kathleen was still serving in the bar when Robert returned, and she hissed, "Where the devil have you been? You were supposed to send a telegram to the Nullagine coppers, not deliver the flippin' thing."

"Shut your bloody mouth, woman," growled Robert. "I did what any decent man would do. I went out to the shack and brought Tobias in."

"You did what? I don't believe you! And where is Tobias now?"

Robert thumbed behind. "Still out in the cart."

"Well, you can't just leave him there! At least show some respect and bring him in."

Robert returned to the cart, but what he hadn't counted on was rigor mortis setting in. Tobias sat in an upright position like a stone statue. Pulling him off the cart, Robert wrapped his arms around his waist and carried him face first into the bar. He called over Tobias's shoulder to Kathleen, "Now what am I supposed to do with him?"

"Well, you can't sit him up at the bar, that's for damned sure. Find him a room and put him in there for the time being."

"I'll put him with The Poet," thought Robert. When The Poet woke the next morning and saw his mate sitting next to him, his hands stretched like claws in front of him, vacant staring eyes and blowflies feeding from the caked blood around his ear, it fair sent him into a bit of a spin.

Dobson had finished his bottle of Muscat. His walk was that of a tired old man as he left the boulder and went to his swag, to sleep and tuck those memories away.

Chapter 16

"I'm tellin' you, Lionel, any lip from her, and I'll be chucking her out along the track," said Harvey, as they loaded Ruby onto the cart.

"It'll be some time before she sobers up, and when she does, give her this," said Gerard, handing up an envelope. "It's her wages and a little extra for a train ticket."

Harvey took up the reins and gave them all a salute, then he was off with Ruby and the bird, which was bouncing about in the back of the cart.

"Okay, boys," said Lionel to the men who had gathered around to farewell Ruby. "She's gone, and good riddance. Now time to be gettin' back to work." He turned to Gerard and said, "Boss, I'll be coming in later. The women want me around when they have a bit of a natter with you."

"That's fine, Lionel," remarked Gerard, then stood watching as the men trooped off to their respective horses. He waited until they had all left before heading back to the homestead, because this was the perfect opportunity for him to begin his search, starting with the office, though he doubted he would find much there, except for Dobson When he entered, to his surprise, Dobson was reclining in a chair with his feet up on the desk. He chuckled as he swung them down. "I heard on the bush telegraph that yer lookin' for a new cook. So I'm lookin' to take the job on."

"I just got rid of one drunk!"

"Well, Billy Muggins, yer got yerself another one. Where does that Bertie keep his grog? I'm parched for a drink."

Gerard gave a shrug. "In a water tank about ten miles from here."

Dobson whacked his hat against his thigh. "Ya know which one?"

"I'm joking," replied Gerard.

Dobson's eyes followed his every move, as Gerard walked around the desk to take a seat.

"Don't yer make no joke about me grog, snorted Dobson. "Anyway, I told Maggie to tell Harvey to pick me up a carton before he went to town and to put it on yer tab."

Gerard just nodded. He changed the subject. "I haven't met the women yet. I was planning on going over to the house to introduce myself."

But Dobson remained single minded and asked shrewdly, "Yer been down the cellar yet?"

"A cellar? I didn't know there was one."

"Yeah, there is. But it's got a dirty big chain and padlock on it. Goes to show how much trust he's got in you, lockin' up the booze box. Did he happen to leave yer some keys? A big brass bastard?"

"Well, yes, he did leave keys," replied Gerard opening a drawer, "but there's definitely not a brass one on the ring." He tossed the keys on the desk. "If you don't believe me, check for yourself."

"Yeah, I believe ya!" Dobson stared moodily at the keys. "Maybe Maggie got an idea where it is." He stood up. "About time I went and gave that woman of mine a bit of slap and tickle, then she'll tell me."

Picking up his swag, he wandered out, leaving Gerard alone to begin his search.

He opened a long cupboard and began piling ledgers on the desk, then meticulously inspected the cupboard for any secret little hideaway drawers. Nothing! He checked behind the cupboard, only to find it bolted to the wall. Placing the ledgers back in the cupboard, he put his weight behind the heavy oak desk and pushed it across the room. He checked for any loose floorboards, but again nothing. Not that he was expecting to find anything so easily, because his gut instinct told him so.

Next, he removed all the framed pictures from the wall and checked the back of each. Then the wall itself. He was putting the room to rights when he heard children's laughter drifting in. Closing the door behind him, he walked around the veranda and in the direction of the children's voices to see them all battling to push a wheelchair across the rough ground.

Sitting in the wheelchair was obviously Emma, but his eyes flashed from her to a boy swinging out on a rope from a nearby tree.

He called a warning, then rushed forward and grabbed the boy mid-air before he collided with the chair. "Got you!" he shouted. He put the boy to the ground. "Next time you do that, you'll have my boot up your bum!"

Emma laughed and held out her hand. "It wouldn't be the first time Burri has sent me flying out of the chair. And by the way, I'm Emma."

Gerard gazed down into a porcelain face that was framed with long, dark hair. She had the most amazing eyes he had ever seen, and when he took her hand, he felt his senses quicken. It was a hand he never wanted to let go, but Emma reclaimed it, using it to encompass with a wave the children who stood shyly by.

"These are the drover's children." she said. "They have a camp a few miles from here and often come in around the homestead to play. Burri you have already met. He's Maggie's grandson."

Emma paused for breath and glanced around at the children. "I think it's time for a cup of tea don't you? I'll have Maggie bring you out some cake, and umm," she looked up at Gerard, "can you push me to the kitchen?"

"I can do better than that," said Gerard. He leaned down and scooped her out of her chair, which had the children breaking into hysterical giggles when they glimpsed Emma's petticoat as Gerard swirled her around and carried her to the kitchen.

Dobson gave a hoot. "Well, I'll be blowed away! If it ain't Sir Bleedin' bloody Galahad himself!" He turned to a woman bent over the oven and gave her a slap on the backside. "Oi woman, ya didn't tell me the missus was out and about walkin' with a new fella."

Maggie slammed the oven door closed. She glanced at Gerard, then glared down at Dobson. "Get that bleedin' dirty hat offa yer head and get outta me kitchen."

Dobson grinned, as he tucked his hat out of sight under his seat. "Meet Maggie," he said, "She ain't the best looker around, but she'll do me – for while."

"What rot," remarked Maggie, giving Dobson a gentle clip on his ear. "He's full of the blarney, this man." She waved the cooking ladle at Gerard, who still had Emma in his arms. "And yer can put the Missus down right there, and yer can go sit over there where I can keep an eye on ya."

Gerard paid no heed to Maggie's curt manner and took an instant liking to her. Without a doubt, she would have her work cut out looking after Emma and that tearaway grandson of hers, thought Gerard. And if that was not enough to keep her busy, he recalled Dobson saying she was also a dab hand at putting broken bones back in place and stitching up blokes when they came in dripping blood all over her kitchen floor.

She was a well-rounded, ample-hipped woman, with her hair plaited and wound around her head, and though she was getting on in years, she had maintained some of her youthful looks. A typical take-charge and a doer, and as Gerard scanned the kitchen, he noticed she had not come over empty-handed. Sitting on the bench were two large cane baskets with food and odd and ends.

Maggie poured boiling water into a large teapot, which she placed near Emma. "You can pour us all a nice cuppa," she said, "and I'll cut up the fruitcake."

She picked up a large carving knife and began slicing.

"I suppose them kids out there will be wantin' some as well," she remarked, as she started piling cakes and biscuits onto a second plate.

Taking the plate, she walked to the kitchen door, opened the fly wire door with her foot and hollered, "Burri! Smoko! Come and get it!"

Burri was tall for eight years, and unlike his grandmother, he was slim hipped and habitually pulled his pants up as they threatened to fall down.

Maggie handed him a plate. "Take this grub out to them kids, and when they be finished eatin', send them lot off home. And don't ya go runnin' off 'cause I need ya 'round here."

Burri didn't look pleased. "Doin' what, Gran?" he asked with a pout.

"Yer can help me, and help this new bloke clean up the friggin' yard. I'm gonna break me bleedin' neck one of these days pushin' the Missus over that lot."

"Aw shit!" he grumbled, as he left the kitchen, "I was gonna meet me mates down at the waterhole and look for taddies."

"That's me grandson, Burri," said Maggie. "And I'm still waitin' for his dad to come back. He went down south drovin' sometime back just after his missus ran off with the cook."

"Has he been gone long?" asked Gerard

"'bout seven years," replied Maggie. "But he's me boy, and he'll be back sometime or other." She lifted lids off pots and stirred a stew that she had put together ready for when the men came in. Satisfied everything was bubbling well, she came and sat down.

Seeing the kitchen as it was now with Maggie putting things to right, Gerard said, "I fail to understand how Ruby managed to keep her position here on the station. An unlikely person to keep as a cook."

"Oh, she was never the cook," interrupted Emma. "She used to be Scherie's nanny. I was away at school at the time of the fire, so I was surprised when I came back and she was still here, considering how much she claimed she hated the place."

Maggie dunked a piece of fruitcake in her tea, savoured it, then swallowed. "All along, I kept tellin' everyone that she and his nibs are in cahoots together. Why else she been hanging' about all these years? Ain't she got a home to go to?"

Emma balled her fists. In frustration, she punched her wheelchair. "And if we don't do something very soon, we won't have a home either. We have to find that marriage certificate. We need it to meet the conditions of the codicils in my father's will. And it's highly unlikely that I can produce a child on such short notice. Scherie is our only answer! That marriage certificate! It has to be somewhere."

But unknown to Emma, she was not the only one who had been searching for the marriage certificate. Bertie had also been looking for it for a number of years.

Chapter 17

Maggie gave the stew a stir, and as she hung up her apron, she said to Dobson, "I got some work to finish back at the house to finish. Keep an eye on me stew 'cause I don't want it stickin' to the bottom of the pot." She then turned her attention to Emma. "And you, missus? Yer sure do look a bit peaked to me, so I reckon a rest will do ya good."

Emma pushed her mug to the side. "I was hoping Lionel would be back by now. But yes, Maggie, I do feel a bit tired. Perhaps I will take a short rest. Can you put me back in my chair, please?"

Emma's voice was tinged with a certain world-weariness. Her world had been confined to a chair with little or no outlet outside of the station to keep her mind occupied. Gerard, however, did not view her as a cripple but as a beautiful vibrant woman who should be running across the paddocks with her hair streaming behind. As he carried her to her chair, he made a commitment to himself: he would do everything in his power to open up her world and make it easier for her to get around independently. And the best place to start was in this yard and make it less treacherous for Maggie to push her around.

Gerard shaded his eyes from the morning sun and watched Maggie disappear around the corner of the house.

"What yer wanna do now?" asked Dobson. "Do some more snooping?"

Gerard dropped his hand. "I've already turned the office upside down and found nothing of particular interest, not that I would expect Bertie to leave an important document such as a marriage certificate framed on the wall."

"Well, yer not the only one that's been huntin' it down. Bertie has as well. Seems no fella around here knows where it got to."

"Well, I'll have to think on it," replied Gerard. He looked around for the children, but they had already gone, and predictably so had Burri. He shrugged his shoulders. "I'll make a start out here," he said. "At least it will fill in a few hours before Lionel comes in."

"Yeah. You do that, bloke. Ya might find a shovel in the old shed out back but," Dobson thumbed to the kitchen, "I'd help ya, but I gotta keep an eye on the stew." Quickly, he spun on his heel and scampered off.

Gerard found the shed and, fighting his way through the cobwebs, found an assortment of gardening tools, many rusted, but they would do the job, thought Gerard, as he dragged them out and gave them a clean. He had done very little gardening in his life, coming from a family that employed people to do such menial work, but Gerard found he enjoyed it – raking, weeding and removing broken stones from the pathway. After a few hours, he looked back on his toil. The garden was now bare but much improved. Deciding he had done enough for the day, he started stacking the gardening tools against the wall.

"What yer doin', bloke?" asked Burri, who wandered over eating a large hunk of damper dripping with condensed milk.

Gerard leaned on the spade. "I heard your grandmother tell you to stay around and give a hand with the garden." Burri gave a sneer. "With everything your grandmother and Emma have done for you," Gerard's tone grew sterner, "don't you think they deserve a little help around the place from you?"

Burri looked abashed. He hung his head, turned then raced off. Gerard continued tidying up and was surprised when some minutes later, Burri returned with a wheelbarrow and a bag of cement.

"We got plenty of this stuff in the back shed," he said, "out by the old house, the one that was burnt down. There's some beaut flat rocks too. I reckon we could make a path for the Missus. What ya reckon?"

Gerard lifted the bag of cement out of the wheelbarrow. "Can you drive a cart?" he asked.

"Sure, I can," remarked Burri proudly. "Old Betsy, she can pull it real good."

"That's good." replied Gerard. "Maybe tomorrow, we can bring some of those rocks in.

"Yeah, I reckon I can find some time. Not many taddies runnin' in the waterhole."

Gerard nodded his head.

"Okay then, tomorrow it is. I'm off to clean myself up." He tousled Burri's hair. "So I'll see you tomorrow," he said with a smile.

After Gerard had washed himself, he gave his clothes a bit of a tub and hung them over the rail to dry. He decided that the best place to wait for Emma and Lionel was in the office. He took his journal with him to pen a few points for discussion, but he found this impossible with his thoughts mainly on Emma. He slammed the journal closed and just sat staring out the door at the hills far off.

"See we got a new yardie," said Lionel, as he pushed Emma into the office. "If yer want, I can spare one of the boys for a few days to help ya clean up."

When Emma was made comfortable, Lionel drew up a chair and pulled out his tobacco pouch. He fingered a fill of tobacco flakes, then rolled a cigarette, while Gerard got straight to the point. "Lionel, give me a brief rundown on the running of this station and what's been happening."

"Well, to begin with," drawled Lionel, as he lit his cigarette, "we ain't finished musterin' yet, but we got more drovers comin' in every day takin' cattle out. Seems to me Bertie don't want one head left standing on the property. Harry Bennett from over Mulligrub Station was tellin' one of the boys he done seen Bertie heaps of times sniffin' around that gold mine that belong to them two old timers. Told Harry he was plannin' on building a house not far from the mine and maybe open up the show."

"And you, Emma," asked Gerard. "Can you add anything?"

"When Scherie was born, I was away at boarding school, so during the time Josephine was here, I know very little, but Ruby would know, as she was Scherie's nanny." Half turning in her chair, Emma looked to the door. "That's strange. I haven't seen her or that bird around today."

"Hopefully, you won't see either of them again." remarked Gerard. "As of this morning, she and that pirate of a bird of hers no longer work on this station."

Emma gave a wide smile. "Maggie's going to be delighted to hear that." She studied the palms of her hands. "Bertie has always hated this station, not like Dad and I. Bertie married against my father's wishes, and he couldn't very well disinherit Bertie, so he made a codicil to his will that High Rocks and Kangaroo Downs could not be sold. They had to be handed down to all future generations, which of course was Scherie, being the only child at the time."

"I can imagine there may be a loophole in that one," remarked Gerard.

"Bertie has a close friend in Perth. A judge. I am more than positive he will take it to a higher court and have it overruled. His friend the judge is as crooked as Bertie. They both have invested interests in brothels in Perth, and that is where he met Josephine." Emma blushed.

"Why would he want to sell the stations, Emma? Do you know?"

"The gold mine. And I can only assume he wants to put it into full operation, and that is going to cost a small fortune to set up." She gave a smile. "He has been foiled on that now. He does not have the lease papers, or at least I don't think he has them. He has to prove that The Poet is legally dead to take over the lease, and that is hard if there is no body to back up that fact."

"And that Bertie," said Lionel with disgust, "has got himself some big bloody gamblin' debts. I know from the past his old man was always bailin' him out of some mess or another."

Emma was near to tears, and Lionel gave her hand an awkward pat. "It'll be all right, missus. Brooding on the past ain't gonna help you sort out the future. Me and the new boss here, well, we gonna help you and yer Uncle Max."

"That flamin' Ruby nicked me plonk from the storeroom," bellowed Dobson, as he barged in on the meeting.

"Hold on, Dobson!" Gerard half stood up, "there was only maybe half a cup left in that bottle."

"Makes no bleedin' difference," retorted Dobson, as he looked wildly around the room. He strode across the room to the gun cabinet, flung open the door and removed a shotgun.

"Where are you goin' with that?" shouted Lionel, as Dobson stomped out the door.

"I'm gonna blow that bleedin' cellar door to smithereens," shouted Dobson. "That plonk bein' good or bad is my bread and butter. It's me flamin' reason for livin'. It's me medicine for me dreams."

Emma laughed. "Let him go. The gun is not even loaded."

Those in earshot joined Emma in the laughter as Dobson stormed out the door.

Seconds later, a loud gunshot reverberated around the homestead that sent the cockatoos nesting in the nearby trees screeching and flying off.

"Well, it never used to be." remarked Emma when the noise died away.

"If there is something to be found in liquid form that smells of alcohol hidden anywhere on this property," added Gerard, "my bet is that Dobson will find it. Come hell or high water."

That evening, when the men came in for dinner and saw the bottles of claret and port on their dining room table, they toasted their new station manager.

However, they were not the only ones regaling their good fortune. Bluey was as well, at the Dawkins Pub, where he dropped in to have a few ales before heading back to High Rocks Station.

He was yarning with Robert. "We got more stores out in that cart than I ever seen in me ten years of workin' out there. Peaches too. We never had peaches before."

"Really!" Robert craned his neck to look out through the door at the cart and saw that, yes, it was loaded down. He plied Bluey with another drink. "So you reckon this manager will stay around?"

"Bloody 'ope so!" Bluey took a long swallow, then wiped his mouth with the back of his hand. "He come up from down Esperance way. For a land bloke, he got some fancy words up his sleeve. Not that he reckons he's better than the next bloke, not like that Bertie."

"Yeah, I have to agree. Bertie is a bit like that. Problem with them cockies' sons, they got too much money. Never had to do it hard like us."

"Perhaps you're right." Bluey snapped his fingers. "Oh yeah. Nearly forgot. Gotta take some bottles of plonk back. Six will be enough."

Robert was surprised. "How come?" he asked. "You usually only take two. What? Is the manager a bit of a slurper 'imself?"

"Nah!" Bluey pulled a ten-pound note from his pocket. "We got Dobson out there."

Robert exclaimed. "And what's Dobson doin' on High Rocks?"

Bluey shrugged his shoulders. "Dunno. He wandered in after the boss left for Perth. Seems Dobson knows the new manager and called by to say g'day. That's all I know."

Bluey took his leave and so did Robert, scuttling across the street to the post office to send the Nullagine Police a telegram.

Chapter 18

"Look, Uncle Max," shrieked Scherie, as she turned the newspaper that she was reading around. "They writin' about our station in the *Headland Miner*."

"That's nice, love. Now eat your egg, or Aunty Jane will be very cross with you," muttered Max, who was engrossed reading about the forthcoming bull sales in the *Bushman's Gazette*.

"Bah!" Scherie tossed her nose up at the egg on her plate. "Where we gonna live later, Uncle Max?" she asked, as she rested her head on the table and picked at the threads of the embroidered tablecloth.

"Live where, Poppet?" mumbled Max

Scherie's freckled brows creased. "When them blokes come 'ere from Port Headland to count how many head we got runnin' on the land."

"Oh. I don't know," Max glanced up. "Ask your Aunt Jane. She knows all about that," he said, then lowered his head to continue reading the article on the bull sales.

"Alrighty, I will." Hopping off her chair, she took the newspaper and raced out the door. Max was relieved. It was nice to have a few quiet minutes, but this was broken with the arrival of Jane.

"Don't you ever listen to this child, Max?" she berated, as she threw the newspaper down in front of him.

"What?" Max glanced up. "But of course, I listen to her dear. That's why I told her to ask you, because you know more about these girl things than I do."

Jane picked up the newspaper and rattled it under her husband's nose. "Bertie has put Kangaroo Downs and High Rocks up for auction."

The news had Scherie wailing loudly. "We not gonna have no humpy no more. We gonna have to live in the bush like Dobson."

"Hush, Scherie!" soothed Jane, placing an arm around the child's shoulder and watching as her husband unfolded the newspaper and read the article. His face was grim when he laid the paper down. "I need to go to High Rocks," he said, and Jane nodded her acquiescence.

He stood up, reached for his hat and, turning, gave his wife a searching look. "Remember about what we have always spoken about?"

Jane bit her lip, nodded and pulled Scherie into a closer embrace.

"So, you know what you have to do," he said curtly. Then giving both Jane and Scherie an awkward hug, he clamped his hat on his head and left.

"Poppet," said Jane with forced cheerfulness. "I want you to go and pack a little bag of clothes. We are going to spend a few days with Aunt Clara at Marble Bar. That will be nice, so go quickly now. I have to get the cart ready."

Scherie looked bewildered and sniffed, "What about your bag, Aunty? Aren't you going to stay with Aunt Clara too?"

"Mine is already packed, dear," she replied. "It's been packed and ready for such a long time," she said to her herself, as she hurried over to the stables.

Jane brought the cart around to the front of the homestead, then dashed inside to check on Scherie. She knew she was being paranoid. "But I'm not taking any chances," she thought, as she piled Scherie's red curls up and tied a scarf around the child's freckled face. Then she plonked a floppy hat on her head, making sure it was well pulled down to hide Scherie's face.

Scherie lugged her small bag outside to wait for her Aunt, while Jane went to her bedroom to drag her suitcase out from under the bed.

Opening it, she rifled through until she found a large leather document holder. She carefully checked the papers inside, then delved into a zippered compartment of the suitcase until her hand felt the cold metal of the small handgun that had been hidden there. She took it out and slipped it into the deep folds of her pocket.

At breakneck speed, Max galloped across the plain. He knew the men from High Rocks were still mustering out at the Ten Mi. He needed to speak with Lionel first, then he would deal with that nephew of his. "I'll kill the little bastard!" he cursed loudly, his words lost to the wind.

The mustering camp was bedlam with clouds of red dust rising from the cattle being moved around. Stockwhips cracked the air with ear splitting precision, and cattle dogs ran around in a barking frenzy. A couple of ringers sitting on the holding yard rails were the first to spot the horseman riding into camp hell for leather. A ringer named Squeaker shouted at his mate Bluey, "Ain't that Max from Kangaroo Downs?"

"I reckon so," drawled Bluey, as he slid off the railings. "Reckon Lionel will wanna know."

But Lionel coming out of the cook tent had already spotted Max as he dismounted from his horse that was lathered in sweat. Lionel ambled towards him.

"Is Bertie still around?" asked Max, as Lionel drew near.

Lionel chuckled as he pulled his hat off and dusted it against his leg. "Nope. He must have liked the look of the new manager yer sent across, 'cause he headed off down to the big smoke the day after the fella arrived."

Lionel put his hat back on and walked beside Max, as he led his horse to the only tree around that offered some shade.

"That bloody little mongrel has put the stations up for auction," said Max angrily, as he tethered his horse and pulled the saddle down.

"Has he just!" remarked Lionel. He picked up a blackened quart pot lying nearby and beat it loudly. "Smoko," he yelled, and that message was well heard around the camp, with men pulling in their horses and others slowly wandering across to the tent while the dogs slunk off to rest in holes they had dug earlier under the scrubby trees.

They all gathered around the billy, squatting on their haunches drinking sweet black tea.

"Bertie's sellin' up," announced Lionel, as he placed his pannikin on the ground. "Scherie found the advertisement in the *Headland* rag 'bout Bertie wantin' an auction."

"Where does that put you, Max?" asked one of the drovers who had known Max since the days of old when they were both young'uns and all chasing the same woman or the same dreams.

"Not in a good position at all," replied Max. He looked around at the dusty-faced men. A round of grim nods showed they understood, while there were a few muttered curses against Bertie.

"We were reckon' on that bein' on the books!" said a grey headed old timer. "That's why he's been pushin' us to bring in the whole mob. Probably wants to cash in before he pisses off."

"I don't think he's goin' too far," remarked Lionel. He pointed into the distance. "I reckon it's that bloody gold mine he's gonna be sinkin' his money in. Gonna cost a fortune to set it up to full production."

"Well, I reckon The Poet gonna have somethin' to say about that, mate," declared Bluey, as he jabbed the butt of his rollie to the side of his mouth. "The Poet hates that Bertie like no man's business. Can't see he's be signin' nothin' over to him."

"Well, boys, sorry to say, but The Poet isn't around anymore," replied Max. "There was a fire out at his shack, and nothin' was left but some ashes and some bone."

"Poor old bastard." The men who had known him commiserated together.

"That ain't gonna help Max much," said Lionel. He stood up, emptied the dregs of his tea into the red dirt and looked across at the cattle yards. "When's the next mob of drovers due to arrive?"

"Sometime tomorrow," replied Ces. "Why you askin'?"

Lionel tucked his thumbs into his back pocket and rocked back and forth on his heels. "We got 'bout 500 head standin' around. What ya reckon, Bluey?"

"'bout that and some more, most of 'em still unbranded."

"Reckon they can stay that way," replied Lionel. He waved the men to their feet. "Be a shame, won't it, when them drovers come tomorrow, and we ain't got a head in the yards, what with them fellas leavin' the gates open tonight and that mob just headin' bush again."

"Yeah, real shame…" said a few of the men in unison, as they walked slowly back to the yards. "Real shame and all."

Chapter 19

Nullagine really had no need for a local newspaper, not when they had Mavis Simons, a bird-like woman with a prominent beak nose who ran the Nullagine Post Office.

Charlie Dwyer, who ran the local store and who had once been sweet on Mavis, entered the post office. A bell jangled loudly as he opened and closed the door, and Mavis glanced up from the telegram she was reading that had just come in from the publican at Dawkins.

"Any mail for me today, Mavis?" asked Charlie, as he walked towards the counter. Mavis reached behind and ferreted out three letters. She handed them over. "There's one is from your daughter Ruby down at Three Springs, and this is a bill yer ain't paid yet. This is a church notice from the Holly Roller Stoner."

"What Ruby got to say, then?" asked Charlie turning the envelopes over.

"Your grandson Michael's got the mumps. Hasn't been to school for ten days," and having been caught out for reading Charlie's mail, she blushed. To cover her gaff, she fanned her face with the telegram. "You goin' past the cop shop?" she asked quickly.

"Can do," replied Charlie "What ya got for them?"

"This telegram just came over from that publican over at Dawkins." She gave a disdainful twitch of her nose. "The sergeant has been tryin' to track old Dobson down for that murder at The Ridge, and Robert Dawkins says he's been hidin' out at High Rocks Station."

"Crikey," said Charlie. "Well, that is important news. Best I get it over to the sarge quick smart then!"

"One second," said Mavis, as she folded the telegram in half and placed it inside an envelope. She licked it down and declared importantly, "Now don't you go tellin' anybody about this because I'm not supposed to be gasbagging' about police business. I took the oath, ya know."

"Oh, you have my word on that, Mavis," replied Charlie, taking the envelope. "I'll not mention one word to anyone, and I promise you, the sergeant will have it in a matter of minutes."

"Have what?" asked Kate Dembon, who had just entered the post office with a parcel she wished to send to her sister in Sydney.

Mavis's beaked nose rose a few inches.

"I am not in a position to discuss the contents of the telegram. It's important police business," she said. Both women waited for Charlie to take his leave. When the jangle of the bell died away, Mavis leaned forward over the counter, as did Kate.

"I can tell you this, though," said Mavis importantly. "That dirty old man Dobson… The law is after him this time, and they know where he be hidin'."

"Really!" Kate Dembon's eyebrows rose higher, as she placed her bulky parcel on the counter. "Why, only just last week, I heard that Dobson stole a lot of money from some miners. They ran him out of town, they did and all. Are the police after him for that? It must be very important if someone is sending telegrams."

"I can't tell you," remarked Mavis, with a sniff. Her mouth pinched into a tight line. "But if you promise to keep it to yourself, I can say this." Mavis looked around the pokey little post office. She lowered her voice to a whisper. "It's murder this time. He murdered some poor old soul up at The Ridge. Took his life's savings. Five bob it was. Can you imagine that? Five bob! I say the man should hang for his wicked crimes."

"Oh, quite right you are there, Mavis," replied Kate, as she handed over a shilling. "Send this off, will you, dear?" Then she hurried out the door to spread the word that the dirty old swagman Dobson had murdered three people for the price of a pint of ale.

Betty Culleton owned the local Nullagine Drapery. She was a good-hearted woman, salt of the earth, with little time for gossip, and when Charlie came through the door, she placed aside a large pair of scissors that she used for cutting calico.

"Reg around?" Charlie asked, as he weaved his way around bolts of material stacked up along the counter and upright in old cut off kerosene drums around the shop.

"He's out the back feeding the chooks," replied Betty, with a heavy-hearted sigh as she pushed her glasses further up the bridge of her nose. "If you like, go out back and put the kettle on. I have a nice batch of scones that just came out of the oven." she offered.

But even the thought of fluffy scones did not deter Charlie from his mission, and he walked around the counter, then disappeared through the door leading to the living quarters behind the shop.

Reg Culleton was scattering grain to the chooks when Charlie came down the back steps. Reg hailed him over with a reminder to close the chicken coop gate. The men conferred about the telegram as the hens clucked away around their feet.

"I'll send Peter out to the station," said Reg, as he emptied the last of the grain to the ground. "Better warn Dobson that the Johnny Hoppers are out lookin' for him."

Vernon was the officer on duty at the front desk, and taking the telegram from Charlie, he dismissed him with an official nod, though not before opening the telegram to read it. Folding it over and with the importance of a bantam rooster, he left Charlie and marched into the sergeant's office.

Charlie decided to hang around a bit longer, in case he was needed, and waited on a hard wooden bench seat close to the sergeant's half open door.

"Sarge, you have got a telegram from the publican at Dawkins," he heard Vernon say. Then came the deep rumble of the sergeant's voice as he intoned, "So Dobson is at High Rocks Station."

"You want me to bring the horses around, Sarge?" asked Vernon. "It's half a day's ride to High Rocks, I believe, and with the circuit magistrate coming to town next week, we could have this case wrapped up very quickly."

Leaning sideways, Charlie peeked through the crack in the door to see the sergeant pull a file out from under a pile on his desk.

"I don't think we should be so hasty," said the sergeant, opening the folder and slipping the telegram inside. "We need to speak with this Dobson fellow first, because I don't take much stock in what this publican has to say for himself. He was too quick to point the finger."

"Quite right, sergeant."

Charlie, having heard enough, tip toed out the door.

No one in Nullagine could beat Betty's scone-making and her secret she kept close to her bosom. Charlie would have married Betty for her scone-making alone, but instead he had married Cybil, a good woman but passionate about her religion, and really, thought Charlie a little sadly, she should have married the church and become a nun. Not that Charlie minded so much now with the years having crept up, and the physical side of their marriage, as short as it was, did beget their only son Clem. It was Clem who sat opposite him out under the grapevine, cramming his mouth with hot buttered scones topped with Betty's strawberry homemade jam. Reg was pouring himself another cup of tea, and Betty, having shut the shop for lunch, sat on a wooden chair fanning her face with the newspaper and listening to the men talking.

"Pete can't ride out to High Rocks," said Reg. "He's done his ankle in. So, Clem, we want you to ride out there, find Dobson and let him know the local coppers are on their way."

"What's Dobson doin' at High Rocks?" asked Clem, as he reached for another scone. "For sure, he isn't workin'. Man never worked a day in his life. Least that I know about. But I did hear it from Mavis that he's got himself a woman out there. But that's a bit of a tall story, I reckon."

The Reverend Stoner was a happy man. Two days had passed since the burial service of Molly Burrows, a wealthy widow who had left him just a paltry five pounds as a donation to his church. "Gawd's trousers!" he had moaned at the time. Not enough to keep body and soul together. But the Good Lord had now given him compensation for the years he had spent kowtowing to that old harridan. Reaching under his bed, he pulled out a large tin. He pried it open, sniffing the mouldy banknotes within.

Over the years, his white collar had given him license to enter the homes of the parishioners as it was accepted as par for the course that free room and board came with his esteemed profession. And of course, it would have been unheard of to blame the good preacher for the valuables that often went missing during his stay.

Given that he had found the tin in Tom Thumb's room, his heart leapt with fear as the voice within said, "What the Lord giveth Tom Thumb can take away."

The Rev snuck across to the far side of the room, put his ear to the wall and listened. Tom Thumb was still searching for the tin. Stoner tiptoed back and sat on the edge of his bed.

Tom Thumb was not a religious man. Stoner paled at the thought, for there was no bluffing that giant, and for sure, if Tom Thumb could not find his tin, he would come looking, ransacking each room in turn. He could not take the risk of Tom Thumb finding the tin. The money was easily discernible, so he needed to find somewhere safe to hide it, preferably before that blasted damn Mary let loose with her mops, rags and dusting cloths came to clean his room.

Desperately, he looked around his room. On the table next to his inkwell was a stack of envelopes. His eyes suddenly lit up with a foolproof plan. It was so simple, it was laughable. All he had to do was put the money in the envelopes of the cattlemen he knew who were away too busy mustering to come to town to collect their mail, then leave it with Mavis at the local post office. In a few days, he would reclaim his letters from Mavis on the pretext of needing to change the dates for next month's service when Tom Thumb left town.

Feeling well pleased with himself, he fetched the envelopes and distributed the money. The tin he wrapped in his long black coat, the one he used for burials, and placing the good book – his bible – on top, he left the room.

He walked jauntily to the back of the boarding house, and passing by a black oil drum, one used for burning rubbish, he deposited the tin in there, making sure to cover it over with the ashes. "How appropriate," he chortled, as he set off to pay Mavis a visit.

The sergeant and Vernon made their way into the Nullegine Hotel and took a stool up at the bar. They had already struck up a cordial relationship with Thomas Ross, the manager of the hotel, and as Thomas placed two glasses of squash in front of the officers, he raised an enquiring eyebrow. "Maud has made a nice steak pie," he said, though it was really roo, but few could taste the difference.

"Don't tempt me," replied the sergeant. He downed the squash, placed the empty glass down along with threepence, being a token amount for the drinks. "Thomas, you've been around these parts a long time. I just want to ask you a few questions."

Thomas crossed his ankles and placed a striped tea towel on the bar. He liked these two officers.

Unpretentious, and they expected nothing for free, not like the other lot, and the sarge was a fair minded coot. "Ask away, Sarge."

"Off the record, mind. But this Dobson character—"

Thomas slapped the bar and laughed. "Sarge, consider yourself lucky that you haven't met the old rogue yet. No bull."

Leaning forward on his stool, the sergeant rested his elbows on the bar: "Have you known him a long time, then?"

Thomas removed a pack of tobacco from his top pocket, slowly rolled a smoke lit it, then blew a stream of smoke towards the tin roof.

"We go back some ways. He used to work out at Kangaroo Downs, but that was when he was a young fella. He was married then, ya know." Thomas lowered his voice. "His Missus had itchy drawers. Every fella around for miles had a thing for her. A damned beautiful woman. She ran off with some bloke and left that little tucker they had when she was just knee high to a grasshopper, that bein' Kathleen that married that Robert Dawkins."

"Hmm." The sergeant gave that a moment's thought. "So who looked after the child, then?"

"Now, that was when Dobson came undone. He was tryin' to look after her best he could mind, but the local welfare didn't take too kindly to Dobson lookin' after the little girl in the bush. They just rocked up one day and took her. Put her in a home of some kind. Kathleen never forgave the old man for that one."

The sergeant's next query was, "You happen to know a man around Dawkins by the name of The Poet?"

"Not really. But I'll tell ya who can fill yer in. Ronny Moss up at the battery. The one in Marble Bar."

The sergeant and Vernon pulled their tired horses up outside the dusty old building that was the local battery.

They found Ronny, his reading glasses perched on the tip of his nose, weighing gold dust and writing figures in a book. He listened intently to what the sergeant had to say then led them to his office out back.

"I think I may have some information still on record. To begin with," said Ronny, as he opened a long ledger, "The Poet's real name was Daniel Flaherty. Used to mine with a partner."

Ronny flipped back through his ledger.

"Ah yes, here we are." He looked up at the sergeant. "I'm not supposed to be giving out this type of information, but I reckon I'll make this time an exception."

The sergeant grinned. "I'm aware of that, Ronny, but this is after all police business."

Ronny ran a finger down a long list of numbered columns. He raised his eyebrows and whistled under his breath. "Don't take this as gospel, Sarge, but that show they had turned over forty thousand pounds in the last ten years."

"What!" The sergeant stood bolt upright. He turned to Vernon. "Did you hear that?"

Vernon nodded, then scribbled in his notebook.

"And you paid them? In cash, or to the bank?" asked the sergeant.

"Cash. Always cash." Ronny closed the ledger, then locked it back in the safe.

"Do you know if they had a local bank account at all?"

Ronny shrugged his shoulders. "I doubt that very much. These old codgers are very suspicious of banks, you know. The old miners preferred to hide their cash or bury it."

The sergeant swung around. "Come on, Vernon." He turned back to Ronny. "I appreciate your help."

The officers walked out into the glaring heat and made their way to the local post office.

"I've been the Post Master here now for the past five years," said the stout man, "and I can assure you, I have never put a letter in the Dawkins mailbag for no Daniel Flaherty. Maybe you can have a bit of a yarn with the bank manager."

"Now the bank," said the sergeant, but they got a chilly reception from the bank manager there. He was filling in for the usual manager who had gone on holidays to Perth. The temporary manager held everyone in this hick town with total disdain and gave the sergeant a cold long-nosed look of disapproval. His thin neck was entombed in a high starched collar, and his chilly eyes looked out over his pince-nez glasses.

"Sir, without a warrant, I can give you no information regarding any of our customers at this bank."

The sergeant clenched his fists. A warrant would take weeks to execute. Though he felt his temper rising, he remained, much to Vernon's surprise, even tempered. "I am only asking, unofficially, if this man had an account at this bank. After all, this is a police investigation, and the man in question has died."

"Prove it," replied the manager coldly as he escorted the policemen from his office.

"Psst!" whispered the teller behind his iron cage. The sergeant sidled up. "I heard what that excuse for a fart of a manager had to say!" Looking nervously around, he whispered, "I can tell you this, Sergeant, those old codgers never once stepped through this door, and we're the only bank in town."

It was early afternoon, and Kathleen was having a nap when she woke with a start when she heard the heavy tread of her husband's boots as he came stomping down the passage. But there was no escaping him that night. He stood in the doorway, his belt already pulled from his trousers, the buckle end dangling from his hand.

Her body shrank in useless defence, and she protected her head and face, as the belt bit into her, and as he beat her, he raged, "You and your fucken' father."

Molly found her lying on the floor unconscious and covered in blood. It had been a vicious beating; she could tell as she knelt down next to her friend and mopped the blood from Kathleen's face with the hem of her skirt. Kathleen moaned, and Molly, terrified that Robert would return, helped her to her feet.

Half dragging, half carrying Kathleen, Molly made for the back door, and as luck would have it, she found still harnessed and hitched outside the kitchen a small cart belonging to one of the miners. She bundled Kathleen in the back, having no time to think of her comfort as she lay among the shovels and picks.

Molly muttered, as she whipped the tired old horse into a canter, "It's about bloody time that Dobson did something."

Molly knew, even though Kathleen had often begged her silence in regard to the beatings, that he bloody well would know this time.

Chapter 20

Burri came marching past wheeling a barrow full of red dirt, as Gerard, taking a break from shovelling and raking, was resting on the broken wicker chair on the veranda. He sighed as he thought of Emma and fantasized about a life with her out here with a couple of kids running around. He wasn't a man born to the land, but a love for it was slowly seeping into his veins.

His thoughts then turned to the old varmit Dobson! In the short time he had known him, Dobson had turned his well-ordered life around. Idly, he scanned the horizon, his attention caught by a rising ball of dust. He stood up, walked to the edge of the veranda and kept an eye on the horseman who was riding in, galloping fast with his head down. The horseman looked vaguely familiar, and Gerard registered surprise when he recognised Max as he dismounted and tied his horse to a tree.

The kitchen door was flung open, and Maggie ran out, squealing in delight with her arms stretched wide towards Max.

"These two are definitely old friends," mused Gerard, watching as Max gathered Maggie up to give her an embrace. After he placed Maggie back on the ground, her calico apron coated with fine red dust, she hurried back into the kitchen for refreshments, and Max strode to the veranda.

"Gawd," he declared, as he pumped Gerard's hand. "It's been some years since…" He looked around and growled, "By the blazes, what has that boy done with this place?"

"Very little, I would have to say," replied Gerard, offering Max the wicker chair to sit in, but Max was agitated. He could not sit. He paced the veranda then stopped to look over the railing.

"Where's Emma?" he asked, then his head snapped around as Maggie rushed out again carrying a vinegar bottle and two glasses.

"Don't let onto Dobson 'bout me stash," she said, pouring a brandy from the vinegar bottle for Max.

Gerard could see the humour in this and smiled as Max cast a dubious eye over the wicker chair. "I'll take the step," he said, settling down and stretching his long legs out.

"Where's Emma," asked Max again.

"Resting up at the house," replied Gerard. "I can tell Burri to let her know that you are here," he added, even though he would have liked to have gone to tell her himself.

"No, Gerard. Let the girl have some moment's peace. The stations are up for auction," he said quietly.

Gerard lowered himself gingerly into the wicker chair and bit down hard on his lip. A flash of anger darkened his handsome features. "When?" he asked curtly.

"Not too sure, but it will be a quick sale. Everyone knows this land has its own underground water supply. We may run short on a lot of things around here, but one thing Kangaroo Downs and High Rock have is a lot of blasted water."

"That will bring the buyers in," remarked Gerard, "water being far more precious than gold. And speaking of gold, is the gold mine included in this auction?"

"Not to my knowledge. That is still under lease to The Poet," Max, his sense of humour coming to the fore, gave a chuckle. "Bertie is going to have dickens of a time trying to sort that mess out without incriminating himself. Blasted man! For the life of me, I cannot understand why."

"Debts!" said Gerard. "I found some ledgers he had hidden away and a letter from the bank in Perth. They are ready to foreclose on this station. Kangaroo Downs, it seems, is under good management and is debt free. It's obvious his sights are set on that gold mine."

Max stood up. A frown creased his brow as he shoved his hands into his pockets. "I sent Jane into Marble Bar with Scherie. They are safer there with her friend Clara. Where's Dobson?"

"He had a helluva row with Maggie yesterday, so he's gone bush for a few days, but you know Dobson, he'll come wandering back."

"And Emma?" asked Max. "How are you two getting along?"

Gerard half kidded, "Another week, my friend, and I will be ready to read the bands at the local Registry Office."

It was a tearful reunion for Max and Emma. To honour their guest, Maggie cooked a roast, washed down with a first-class bottle of claret brought up from the cellar. As they ate and drank.

Unbeknown to them, Molly had reached the river crossing and was pulling the cart over. She helped Kathleen from the cart, and they appeared as a couple of drunken floozies as they staggered down to the water's edge, where Kathleen collapsed, her skirt billowing out around her.

Lifting her skirt high, Molly tore away her underskirt and cried as she bathed Kathleen, the river running red with the blood of her friend. The shock of the cold water had revived Kathleen, and when she had been cleaned up, she was able to limp back to the cart.

Everyone had gone to bed except for Maggie, who being a night owl sat in the lounge room darning socks. When she heard the crunching of cartwheels outside, she lay her work down and went to the window to look out.

"Who the blazes are these people," she muttered. Then grabbing the Tilly lamp off the hook, she went to stand at the front door.

It was hard to make out who it was, as two figures huddled together walked slowly up to the house, but her face registered her shock to see Kathleen broken, beaten and bleeding. Running down the stairs, she wrapped her arm around Kathleen's shoulder to assist her up and into the house.

"Ouch!" cried Kathleen, as Maggie dabbed iodine on Kathleen's cuts.

"Sit quiet, girl," Maggie told her softly, "I don't want you waking Emma."

"I'm already awake," announced Emma, as she wheeled herself into the kitchen and gasped as she saw the condition Kathleen was in.

"My God in heaven," she cried, as she instinctively reached for Kathleen to give her some measure of comfort. "Who did this to you?"

"Robert," mumbled Kathleen through bruised and swollen lips. "He did this to me."

"He's given her some bad beatings in his time," said Molly, who pulled her shawl tighter around her as she sat at the table with her feet in hot water sipping hot sweet black tea.

Emma's lips were white with anger. "The man should be horsewhipped!"

"And that's what I'm hoping Dobson will do. Least 'fore he kills her," said Molly.

"Both of you will be staying right here with us," said Maggie gruffly, as she parted Kathleen's hair and began dabbing the small holes made by the pin of the belt buckle that were dotted all over her scalp. Kathleen winced, but she was too exhausted to complain. She lay her head on the table listening as Molly recounted the physical abuse by her husband over the past few years.

Chapter 21

Gerard and Max showed the tenderness of two fine gentlemen as they carefully carried Kathleen between them to the spare room that Maggie had prepared. A draught of laudanum had eased a lot of Kathleen's pain, and she looked at peace when Maggie tucked the white crisp sheets up around her.

"I'll sit up with her," offered Burri, who had also been woken when Maggie had roused the men from their beds. Maggie nodded. She gave her grandson an affectionate pat on the shoulder and, turning the lamp down low, quietly closed the door behind her.

They all regrouped around the table. Maggie was concerned for Emma. She looked shocked and pale. Quickly, she refilled her cup with a strong brew of tea. Gerard shook his head when Maggie offered him another cup. He was trying to come to grips with what he had seen, and he shuddered thinking what Kathleen must have endured. Max remembering Kathleen as that wayward child who had sat silent and tight lipped, looking up only when Maggie had sat herself down in a chair close to Emma.

Burri dozed in his chair while Kathleen dreamt of highland hills and sun streaming down as she ran across the green grassed meadow towards the loch of still water. It was warm where she was and she felt safe.

"Kathy," called her beau from long ago. "Come fishing, my love."

Taking his hand, she lifted her velvet skirt and admired her dainty shoes as she stepped into the boat.

"We'll sail away, darling," he said, as he took up the oars. The small boat slipped out onto the water, and as it did, Kathleen's spirit slipped from her beaten body and floated past Burri and out the door.

Dobson gave a loud snort as he rolled over in his swag. He opened one eye and listened to the sounds of the bush around him. He became aware of an unknown presence and, sitting up, he looked out to the horizon.

A new day was dawning, the sun was breaking over the horizon, and the land around was awash in soft hues of pinks and greys. Above him, and for the first time in his life, he saw one white cloud drift slowly across the sky, then dissipate into nothing in front of his eyes. Then he felt it. A pain, sharper than any knife cutting into his heart. His head rolled back, and his cry was that of an injured animal as he tried to call his daughter back.

They brought her back to Kangaroo Downs. It was fitting that the only men in her life who truly loved her and would do her no harm carried her coffin to a grove of trees and laid her to rest beside Max's parents.

Three days after Kathleen had died, those from High Rocks began to talk about returning to the station, but Max took a stand. "I want both Emma and Maggie to remain on Kangaroo Downs," said Max. "This homestead is much better equipped to deal with Emma's needs."

Gerard had to agree with that.

Max gave his niece a fond look. "You'll be doing Jane a favour, Emma. God knows the woman is lonely out here on her own. Not that you ever hear one word of complaint from her."

"I don't want to be a burden to anyone," replied Emma softly.

Max roared, "My God, girl. You get that thought out of your head right now. That's your brother talking!"

He eyed his niece. Since her return to Kangaroo Downs, she had lost that peaked look. There was colour in her cheeks, and she looked stronger than she ever had before. Emma looked to Maggie, who gave her nod of approval. High Rocks was sucking the girl's lifeblood, and Emma was in no position to stand and fight her brother alone. It was no life for Emma on High Rocks. She was always tense when Bertie was near and worried continually. Maggie thought with a little sadness that the time had come for Emma to cut her ties from High Rocks and be given the chance to start a new life. She glanced at Gerard.

Dobson had said little since the death of his daughter, and those around him allowed him his time to grieve.

Dealing with his past made him morose, and he was always making plans in his head that centred on Robert and his painful demise. That kept him going.

"Who the devil is that now?" said Maggie, as she opened the kitchen door and looked out to see a man dismount at the front gate.

Emma wheeled her chair to the door and peered around. "It looks like a policeman," she whispered.

Which it was.

"Good morning, ladies," said the sergeant, as he came strolling up the path. "Sergeant Roberts is my name, and I am from the Nullagine Police."

"What can we do for you, Sergeant?" asked Maggie, giving him a suspicious look that did not go unnoticed by the officer.

"I'm new to the district, which means I spend a lot of my time getting lost around the bush."

Maggie gave a thin smile.

"I am heading to a station they call High Rocks, but it seems I may have taken the wrong turn some miles back. Perhaps you ladies could point me in the right direction?"

Maggie looked wary. "What's your business on High Rocks, Sergeant?" she asked, and her head snapped up as she saw Dobson coming along the veranda. He, seeing the policeman, sidled into the first open doorway, then scurried out through another door, before taking off up to the back shed, where Max and Gerard were busy hitching up a cart to take to High Rocks to bring Emma's belongings back to Kangaroo Downs.

"Ya got that bleedin' copper from Nullagine on yer flamin' doorstep," said Dobson, as he came into the shed with his swag dangling over his shoulder.

Gerard jumped off the back of the cart. Seeing Dobson's face, he thought that the arrival of the law was timely. If anything, it had certainly brought back Dobson's sassiness.

"For sure, the bastard is lookin' for me for pinchin' bar change. I reckon I'll be headin' bush for a few days." He turned, then turned back around again. "Oh yeah, forgot to tell ya, Max. You'll be needin' a few quid for that auction comin' up. If yer happen to pass by the cemetery at Dawkins, take a shovel with ya mate. There are about eighty thousand quid in Tobias's box. That should do ya to get ya outa the shit."

Then Dobson was gone, doing what he did best, scurrying off into the bush.

Max and Gerard returned to the homestead. The sergeant was at the kitchen table, a plate of cake in front of him, along with a large mug of steaming black tea. Maggie was entertaining him, telling him the secrets of her poppy seed cake.

Max opened the door, and both men stepped through, hanging their hats on the hooks along the wall.

"Max Huntingdale," said Max extending his hand. The sergeant half rose. "And this is," he said, thumbing to Gerard, "Peter Watkins, my station manager. So, what can I do for you, Sergeant?"

Max lowered himself into a chair, and Gerard moved across to the stove. Keeping his back turned to the sergeant, he began tidying up the wood box.

Emma sat quietly in her chair chopping up vegetables. Maggie began to prattle.

"The sergeant has lost his way," she said. "Headin' to where? High Rocks?"

The sergeant nodded.

"Well, I already told him he needin' to go another mile or so along, up past Muligubs then at the old tree, yer gotta head West for another mile or so. Ain't that right, boss?"

"Yes, you're right, Maggie," replied Max, as he took up a piece of cake. "But there's a quicker way to get to High Rocks. You are about thirty miles out of your way, Sergeant, but I'll point you in the right direction… that is, when you've finished your cuppa."

Now that the wood was neatly stacked, Gerard sauntered out of the kitchen and waited for Max around the corner of the homestead. Within a few minutes, both men appeared, and together, they walked to where the sergeant's horse was tethered. Gerard couldn't hear what Max was saying, but by the direction he was pointing, even Gerard knew that the sergeant was being directed back to Marble Bar. The long way back.

Chapter 22

Max and Gerard followed along behind the cart, and as the horses walked at their own leisurely pace, the man talked, debating why the sergeant from Nullagine would be tracking Dobson down. "Maybe it is for pinching change," said Max.

"I doubt that very much," replied Gerard "The sergeant wouldn't come this far afield for such a petty crime. Maybe it was about the grog he pinched from a man named McIntyre, or for stopping that government train."

"What about murder and arson?" said Max. He cast a look at Gerard. "Now that would warrant a station call, don't you think?" Max urged his horse into a trot. "Whatever it was, the last thing we need is the sergeant looking over our shoulders."

It was late afternoon when they arrived back at High Rocks. Burri tended to the horses, while Gerard and Max checked the homestead in the event of unlikely intruders, but everything was as they had left it on the day they had taken Kathleen home.

Without the women around, the homestead was cheerless. Even the chooks looked unhappy, thought Gerard, as he offered them a bucket of mouldy scraps, but things were going to be better, he told them, as they listlessly pecked at the food, when he moved them to Kangaroo Downs.

"We'll be batching for a few days," said Max that night, as he dished up a plate of watery stew. "I'm not much of a cook," he added, handing Gerard a spoon to eat with, "but we won't starve."

After dinner, they talked long into the night, and before they fell into their beds, they both agreed that taking up Dobson's generous offer of eighty thousand pounds was a sensible one.

At least Max would have some folding cash when the stations came under the hammer, they figured. But they came up with no immediate solution to proving Dobson's innocence in regard to the death of The Poet.

Dobson had made more than a mile down the track. He lay his swag on the ground and peered through the bushes towards the men camped around a campfire. There was no mistaking the hulk of Tom Thumb sitting on the back of the cart and the darting figure of The Weasel as he ran around doing Tom Thumb's bidding.

"Well, if it ain't the Swagman," said Tom Thumb when Dobson broke through the bushes and walked into camp. "Ya know the coppers are after ya? After us too, but I pay no mind to them."

Dobson dropped his swag. He got straight to the point. "Ya got any grog around?" he asked

"Sure have," replied Tom Thumb. "Hey Weasel, we got company. Break open a flagon or two."

A flagon apiece the men drank. Tears rolled down Tom Thumb's cheeks when he was told about Kathleen, which was followed by a loud bout of hiccups.

The Weasel crunched his knuckles. "That rotten maggot Robert won't be getting' away with that," he declared hotly, then broke into song, "Take me home, Kathleen."

After a number of renditions, the men put their heads together and devised a plan of Robert's forthcoming and unfortunate accident. The three agreed the best plan was to tie the bastard to the bed, douse his room and the pub in kerosene and burn him and his pub to the ground. With that being his last thought for the night, Dobson slept well.

There was not a brick left unturned, not a nook or cranny that was not investigated. Every mattress in the house had been ripped open in search of anything that would tie Bertie to his heinous crimes. But Max and Gerard had come up empty-handed, and when their search was done, they sat despondently around the table drinking more than a drop of Bertie's Scotch whisky.

Gerard, stretching, leaned back in his chair, folded his arms behind his head and considered their options.

"I think the best thing, Max," he said, "is if we take a ride into Dawkins and visit the cemetery bank. We don't want to leave things to the last minute, and I think it would raise a great deal of suspicion if we pulled up at the auction with a coffin in the back of the cart."

"Well, it would certainly set some tongues wagging. No doubt about that," replied Max. "It'll have to be at night that we go."

"Agreed." Gerard stood up and gave a stretch. "You know the gravesite, of course?" he asked.

Max blinked a number of times. "No. I have no idea, but I'm sure it will have a headstone and should be easy to find."

"Pity we don't have Dobson with us. But he's got his own demons to deal with at this time," Gerard added.

The following night, the grave robbers prepared their cart. Picks, shovels and ropes they thought would do the job, and with Max taking up the reins, they set off into the night. Max did not want to rouse anyone's suspicions, and on the outskirts of town, he instructed Gerard to pull the collar of his coat up and pull his hat well down over his face.

"We are well disguised, I think," said Gerard, as he buried himself well down into his coat, while Max kept his head down and hunched himself over.

Despite their efforts, the few people out on the street at such a late hour hailed Max heartily as the cart made its way along the street and past the Dawkins Pub.

"This is it," said Max, guiding the cart into the cemetery. "We'll pull up and," he cursed, as the cart rocked sideways, "what the hell was that?"

"I think you just ran over someone's headstone," said Gerard.

Gerard hopped from the cart and peered at the broken tombstone lying on the ground. He read the inscription, pieced the broken stone together and asked in a hushed whisper, "Does Daisy May Hawkins ring a bell?"

"She used to be the doctor's wife," whispered back Max. Leaning down, he pulled up a kerosene lamp and handed it down to Gerard. "Be careful you don't tip it up. Not much kero left in it, I'm afraid."

He clambered from the cart. "Now where to start?" he said, looking around in the night. He gave his eye time to adjust to the darkness, and when he could ascertain the outline of headstones and a few angels, even one with a broken wing, he pointed to that particular row. "We'll start here," he said.

He lit the lantern, adjusted the flame and began walking along the row, with Gerard reading out aloud the names of the dearly departed. They walked up and down, then retraced their steps a number of times, but damned if they could find the grave that held Tobias's fortune.

Tired, they both sat down atop of Henry John Smith and his dearly loved wife Gertrude, who was the mother of seven and grandmother of twenty-one.

"Dearly missed, she is," said Gerard.

"Who wouldn't be with, how many nippers did you say she had?"

Gerard checked again. "Twenty-one, but it looks a bit faded to me. Maybe it is twenty-nine."

Max scratched his chin. "Well since you're on such intimate terms with this family, ask Gertie where that blasted Tobias is buried, will you?"

Max came to his feet and began walking slowly along the line of graves.

"In an unmarked grave," called out Gerard, who, leaping to his feet, trotted to catch up with Max. "In an unmarked grave," he repeated.

Max, bent over reading another inscription, asked, "Did Henry or Gertie tell you that?"

Gerard encompassed the graveyard with a sweep of his hand. "It just came to me. We know the box is definitely here somewhere. We've double checked all the graves, and we can't find a tombstone with Tobias's name on it, or even one close to that, so that coffin has to be an unmarked grave."

Max dug the shovel into the ground. "Well, damned if you may be right. And don't forget, Dobson did say he had recently been here, so we have to look for some freshly dug up ground."

The first plot of freshly dug ground uncovered an old timer who lay in his coffin in a crumpled suit with his hands folded over his chest.

"Leave him there," said Max, as he swung the pick back into another plod of ground. "We'll bury him later."

Taking turns, Max and Gerard swung that pick, and when six coffins dotted the cemetery, they finally struck gold on the seventh.

It took time and muscle power to lift the steel coffin out, but finally they did and collapsed from sheer exhaustion over the top. They stayed like that, panting and gasping, for some minutes. When Max had recovered his breath, he took hold of the crowbar that they had found in the grave along with a couple of empty flagons and walked slowly around the coffin.

"Pretty bloody fancy," he commented, as he wedged the crowbar in. At that precise moment, the lantern flickered and ran out of kerosene, and the men were left standing in pitch darkness.

"We'll have to take the coffin back to the station and open it there," said Max. "It's not possible to do it in the dark."

"Shit!" cursed Gerard. He doubted ten men could carry that box, which enlightened him. "And that is where Tom Thumb came in."

Gerard scouted around to find a couple of stout wooden boards while Max pried the lid off one sturdy coffin. They set up a ramp, and even then, with the use of ropes, it took an hour to load the coffin up onto the cart.

When the job was done, Max began searching for the shovel to fill the graves in. Then it happened. A loud explosion rocked the foundations of the small town of Dawkins. Balls of fire ignited the pub, belching flames high into the sky.

Opened mouthed and in shock, Max and Gerard looked at each other.

Max found voice first. He ran to the front of the cart to stop the startled horse from bolting, shouting, "Has to be bloody Dobson!"

Chapter 23

It took three days before the last glowing ember extinguished, and all that was left of the Dawkins Pub was a pile of soldering rubble.

The people of Nullagine and Dawkins were in an uproar. They had hunted the sergeant to ground, and he now sat at his desk weeping, Vernon comforting him.

"My superiors assured me that this was going to be an easy posting," he howled, adding another wet hanky to the pile accumulating on his desk. "The most you'll get is a Saturday night brawl, they said." The sarge looked up at his underling with a tear-stained face. "And what have we got? A missing miner, his burnt down shack, a crazy hobo running amuck in the bush, six coffins sitting out of their graves at the cemetery – one gone missing – and a pub that went up in a ball of flames. I just can't take it anymore." The sarge wailed loudly.

"Now now, Sarge," consoled Vernon, who had never seen a man have a nervous breakdown until now. "I'll get you a nice mug of warm milk. That'll help you."

Vernon went to another room, where the potbelly stove was. He stoked it with dry tinder, placed a small pot of water on it, added a few spoons of powdered milk and hummed as he waited for the milk to warm.

"Dobson said nothing about cash," said Gerard, as he double counted the piles on the desk. The gold they put into sacks. Burri was dragging the last one across the floor, where he stacked it up against the wall with the others. Max could only shake his head back and forth in wonderment. He would have to work three lifetimes over to attain such wealth, and Gerard had already calculated that there was enough money and gold to buy both stations outright.

"What worries me," said Max, "is how am I going to pay all this money back? It really isn't my money."

"It's hard to pay a dead man back," said Dobson, as he stepped into the room.

"Dobson!" cried Max and Gerard in unison.

"Yeah, it's me, unless I got a twin hangin' around some place. Now that'd be a laugh. Two of me for youse all to deal with."

Max came to his feet. He looked sternly at his old friend. "Don't tell me you had anything to do with the Dawkins Hotel burning down, Dobson."

"Then I won't tell ya," replied Dobson shortly. He eyed the stacks of money on the table. "Reckon yer got enough to see ya through, Max?" he asked.

Gerard laid his pencil down and closed the notebook that he had been doing his calculations in.

"As a matter of interest Dobson," asked Gerard, "you have known all along about this little haul, yet you've never taken a penny?"

Dobson smiled, the first since the death of his daughter Kathleen. "It's one of me principles ya reckon'd I didn't have, Nancy." He flapped his hand, embarrassed at being caught out. "Aw shit! If I had money in me kick, it'd take all the fun out of me life."

"And The Poet?" Gerard's face registered his confusion, since for the life of him, he could not fathom the logic of some of these old timers. "All this caboodle." Gerard picked up a pile of the mouldy notes and let them slip out of his hand. The notes fluttered down onto the table. "And the Poet lived out his days hand to mouth. I just don't understand."

Dobson shrugged his shoulders and looked searchingly around the room. "You wouldn't, so don't waste yer time tryin' to nut that one out. We got any grog left on this station?"

"I'll get you a drink," said Max, but before he did, he rested a hand on Dobson's shoulder, "You've always been a true friend. You know that, Dobson?"

"Well, a good mate wouldn't leave another mate hangin' out for a drink," grumbled Dobson. "Now git yer arse down to that cellar, Max," he added with a laugh.

While Max was raiding the cellar, Burri returned, having left unnoticed when Dobson had turned up. Burri tossed a leather satchel on the table. "I found this in the lid of the coffin. Maybe it's important or something. I dunno."

Gerard raised his eyebrows in surprise. He undid the leather thongs and turned the satchel upside down, emptying the contents onto the table. Systematically, Gerard checked every document. "Wonders will never cease," he said to Dobson.

"I had no idea!" exclaimed Dobson. He backed away "And ya gotta believe me, Nancy."

"I believe you," laughed Gerard. "Sit down and take a load off your feet, mate"

Max returned carrying a couple of dusty bottles. "A bottle of sherry and some port for you Dobson. There's not much left, but I'll let you into a little secret. Maggie's got her own stock… Brandy. Bottled in vinegar bottles."

"Bleedin' woman! Bet she's been drinking a few on the side." Dobson vacated his chair and pushed it close to Max. "I reckon ya need to sit down but 'fore yer do, you'll probably be needin' a good drop of vinegar 'yerself."

Handing Dobson the bottle of sherry, Max asked: "What do you mean I'll need something stronger to drink? If it's bad news, tell me tomorrow."

Gerard lifted the notebook up to disclose a pile of papers underneath. He lay the book to the side and picked up a thick document, showing Max as he did the two red wax seals on the last page. "This is the mining lease."

Max's mouth dropped open. His eyes widened in surprise. "It's the what?"

Gerard kept his eyes locked on Max. His tone was even. "Yes, it's the mining lease, Max."

He handed it over and picked up another document. He held it in the air between his thumb and forefinger. "This is Tobias's birth certificate."

He placed the document down.

Picking up the last three documents, he waved them in the air as if he was drying wet ink. "This is your father's Last Will and Testament. You can read it later, but it was drawn up shortly before your brother died. And what I have here," Gerard raised a piece of paper high over his head, "is Scherie's birth certificate and," he casually tossed the last document across the table, "Bertie's wedding certificate to her mother Josephine Brooks."

"Oh my God," declared Max, collapsing back in his chair. He needed a few seconds to recover from the shock. His head dropped down. How many years had they searched? How many years had Emma endured her brother's humiliation, and all this time, they had been buried for safekeeping.

Chapter 24

Max and Gerard decided it was time to go out and check out the gold mine, with Dobson inviting himself along, but Burri opted to remain at the homestead, for he was keen to get Emma's house packed up and shift her to Kangaroo Downs. He worked tirelessly through the morning. Around noon, he left Emma's house and wandered over to the main homestead to raid their food safe. He wasn't one to complain, but he was missing his grandmother's cooking. It had been decided that Max, Dobson and Gerard would take turns at cooking, but Burri thought that none of them could even fry an egg. Max's specialty was watery stew, and Gerard's was pancakes, thick ones, half cooked through, a real doughy mess that stayed glued to the palate for hours. Dobson proved to be the best cook. He could really throw a meal together, but only if you liked snakes. Its meat was a bit chewy, but the spuds were good, charcoaled spuds that he threw into the campfire and left to roast until the outer skins were black and crunchy.

From the kitchen safe, Burri took the last of the damper, buttered it and taking a mug of water wandered outside to eat his lunch. He was feeling dozy. He rested his head up against the veranda post and quickly nodded off. He wasn't sure how long he had slept, but the front gate banging jolted him awake. "Must be them blokes returnin'," thought Burri. Then he became alarmed when he did not recognise the footsteps of two men coming up the garden path.

Jumping from the veranda, he blocked the path of two big policemen.

Sitting at the kitchen table, Burri kept his head down, mumbling incoherently when the coppers tried to engage him in conversation. His sense of relief was enormous when finally he heard the men return, and the sound of Max's voice was reassuring.

Max was the first to enter the kitchen, and he gave a start to see they had visitors.

"So we meet again, Mister Huntingdale," said the sergeant seated at the table nursing a mug of tea as well as a bruised ego. When Gerard stepped through the doorway and stood next to Max, the sergeant's eyes lit up. "And look who we have here," he remarked, eyeing Gerard coldly, "Mister Watkins, the station manager from Kangaroo Downs, I believe."

"Just our bloody luck," muttered Max under his breath.

Then the sergeant's face suffused with colour when he heard Dobson, coming up the rear, shouting, "We got any grog left, or do we gotta crack open them vinegar bottles?

Oh fuckin' shit," he cursed to see the company sitting at the table. "If it ain't the Johnny Hoppers from Nullagine."

"Ah, Mister Dobson. We meet again," said the sergeant, rising out of his chair like the phoenix from the ashes. He pointed at Dobson, "One warning, Mister! You take a runner this time, Mister Dobson, and I'll be locking up your friends here for a very long time."

Having had a lot to do with coppers in his time, Dobson knew one who meant business when he met one. He slid down on his chair and dragged his felt hat off his head.

"Now Sarge," he whined, "me friends 'ere have done nothin' wrong, and if ya reckon they have, or ya been stickin yer beak in around the place and found some things that's none of yer bleedin' business, or this kid 'ere," he looked at Burri, "said somethin' he shouldn't then yer, just lock me up. This lot got no idea 'bout what's goin' on round 'ere."

The sergeant remained silent. He raised his craggy eyebrows.

Dobson squirmed in his seat. He wet his lips nervously and looked as guilty as hell.

"Well, ya gonna tell me what's goin' on then, Sarge," he snapped. "Because if ya don't tell me what's been goin' on, then I could be incriminating meself for somethin' I never done in the first place."

The sergeant's hand slowly snaked out across the table. It curled around Vernon's pencil. "Constable, if you don't stop your infernal scribbling and put that fucking pencil away, I'm going to jam it up your arse."

Gerard's own buttocks twitched at his own memory of a branch up the arse. He quipped, "Dobson's good at that."

The sergeant's eyes narrowed. "Mister Ward. I strongly advise you to keep your mouth shut, otherwise I will personally ensure that the next article you write is about prison life and that will be from your own experience from the inside."

Max's jaw tightened. He blustered indignantly. "Right. Now you listen to me, Sergeant. You have arrived here unannounced," he said.

The sergeant jumped in. "I wouldn't say that, Mister Huntingdale! I believe it was you yourself in actual fact that gave me directions to High Rocks Station."

Max tried a winsome smile, but it did nothing to soften the sergeant's stoney expression. "Gee, Sarge," replied Max, with a sheepish look. "Sure took your time getting here. Did you get lost?"

The sergeant waved to a chair. "Now, you take a seat Mister Huntingdale. I think it's high time we all had a little chat about some very unusual events that have been occurring around the district."

Over numerous pots of tea, the sergeant did his interrogation, with Vernon occasionally putting in his two bobs' worth as he peeled spuds for the evening meal.

He had come across some tins of corned beef in the storeroom, but he fretted over the spuds, because they were soft and a bit old. He decided if he mashed it all in with the corned beef, added a pinch of this and that from Maggie's spices, it would be tasty enough, and no one would really mind. He just hoped it was going to be enough. There was no pudding to follow. He looked over his shoulder and pulled the oven door slightly open. His damper was rising beautifully. Like it or lump it, they would just have to fill up on that. When dinner was over, Burri helped the constable with the dishes, and Max went to the storeroom, returning with three bottles that were uncorked. Meanwhile, Dobson sat, looking dark and vowing that woman of his was gonna be getting a real tongue lashing from him for hidin' his grog in those vinegar bottles sitting on the table.

When the sun came up next morning, they were all still grouped in the kitchen talking, all that is except for Burri and Vernon, who were curled up on the floor sleeping soundly. Bleary eyed and heavily whiskered, the sergeant pulled himself to his feet. Now that he had all the facts, he felt more in control of the situation, and even though the story that had unfolded through the night was bizarre beyond belief, he could nevertheless work with it. But right now, he was going to find himself a bed and have a few hours' sleep. A suggestion, he said, that the others would do well to follow.

THE END